"H... ...u,
Lady Emma?

"Have we met before? I do not think the memory of you lingers from England, somehow...."

Desperate to take his mind from recollection, she locked her hand on his and asked him to dance, completely ignoring the look of astonishment on his face.

Asher's body melded against her own and he found the rhythm of the music with much more finesse than she did. Leaning into him for just a moment, she closed her eyes.

Wishing.

Wishing that she was a wellborn lady and that he might like her just a little. Wishing that things could have been different between them and that all he believed of her was true.

* * *

High Seas to High Society
Harlequin® Historical #888—March 2008

Sophia James

HIGH SEAS TO
HIGH SOCIETY

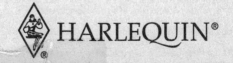

HARLEQUIN®

TORONTO • NEW YORK • LONDON
AMSTERDAM • PARIS • SYDNEY • HAMBURG
STOCKHOLM • ATHENS • TOKYO • MILAN • MADRID
PRAGUE • WARSAW • BUDAPEST • AUCKLAND

ISBN-13: 978-0-373-29488-6
ISBN-10:   0-373-29488-3

HIGH SEAS TO HIGH SOCIETY

Copyright © 2007 by Sophia James

First North American Publication 2008

This edition published by arrangement with Harlequin Books S.A.

® and TM are trademarks of the publisher. Trademarks indicated with ® are registered in the United States Patent and Trademark Office, the Canadian Trade Marks Office and in other countries.

www.eHarlequin.com

Printed in U.S.A.

For Pete, my pirate!

Chapter One

London, May 1822

Asher Wellingham, the ninth Duke of Carisbrook, stood in a corner with his host Lord Henshaw, and watched a woman sitting alone near the dais.

'Who is she, Jack?' he asked with feigned casualness. In truth he had noticed her as soon as he had walked into the salon, for it was seldom a beautiful woman wore such a plain gown to a ball and then sat alone looking for all the world as if she was actually enjoying her own company.

'Lady Emma Seaton, the Countess of Haversham's niece. She arrived in London six weeks ago and every young blood has tried to strike up some sort of relationship with her since.'

'Arrived…from where?'

'Somewhere in the country, I would presume. Obviously she has not seen a London stylist—I've never seen hair quite like it.'

Asher's gaze travelled across a thatch of blonde curls barely restrained by hairpins. A home-fashioned coiffure, he surmised, and executed badly, yet the whole effect of sun-bleached curls threaded with gold and corn was unsettling.

People seldom surprised him. Or intrigued him.

But this girl with her lack of self-consciousness and her fashion faux pas had succeeded. What woman, after all, ate her supper whilst wearing her gloves and licked the end of a silk-covered finger when the jam of a sweet biscuit stained it.

This one did.

Aye, this one did not nibble on the food as every other female in the room was wont to do, but piled the plate before her from the tray of a passing waiter as though her very life depended on it. As though it might indeed be a good deal of time until the next course showed itself, or as if, perhaps in her old life, in some country village, she had not had as much food as she had needed and could barely believe that she was being offered such bounty here.

He saw others looking her way and felt vaguely irritated. The buzz of whisper had grown as she stood, tall and thin, the hem of her gown reaching a good inch above the line that would have been decent and at least three inches above the length that was now in vogue.

He could hear the conjecture and the whispers all around, even if she did not seem to, and he wondered why the hell it should concern him anyway, but there was something about her. Some hint of familiarity.

Some elusive memory of fellowship that could not quite be shaken. How could he know her? He tried to determine the colour of her eyes, but from this distance he could not. Turning, he cursed the Countess of Haversham for being remiss in seeing to her niece's wardrobe and hairstyle, and left Lady Emma Seaton to the circling society wolves.

The room was crowded with men and women chatting at great speed and without pause, the music from a stringed quartet hardly discernible across the din.

Emerald frowned and sat, closing her eyes in order to listen better. People here did not seem to appreciate music, did not seem to understand that, when silence threaded the undertones, sound could be better heard, melody enhanced.

The music was unfamiliar, an English tune and lightly woven. She could almost feel her harmonica at her lips, notes soft across whisper-swelling seas. Jamaica crowded in like an ache.

Nay, she mustn't think of this, she admonished herself, drawing her body more upright in the chair and forcing herself to observe the pressing crowd around her.

This was her life for a time.

England.

Her hands fingered the silk gown that swathed her from head to foot and, raising the third glass of fine champagne to her lips, she swallowed quickly. Good drink dulled her anxiety and heightened other senses. Sound. Smell. Feel. Every pore in her body longed for sun or wind or rain upon it, to break free of her high-waisted frilled bodice. To lie on summer-warm sand or in the wild grasses on the rise above Montego Bay or to dive deep into an azure sea, down and down until the bubbles tickled greenness and the other world was lost.

Letting out an audible sigh, she schooled her thoughts. 'No more memories,' she whispered beneath her breath and was pleased when her aunt sat down on the spare seat opposite. The paleness in her face, however, was alarming.

'Are you quite well, Aunt?'

'He is here, Emmie…' Miriam could barely enunciate the sentence.

'Who is here?' She knew which name she would hear even before her aunt spoke.

'Asher Wellingham.'

Panic raced across fear and anger.

Finally, he had come.

Weeks of waiting had strained her nerves almost to breaking point and the advances of the men here had become increasingly more difficult to discourage. But had he seen her? Would he remember?

Placing her glass upon the table, she refused more from a circulating waiter and her hand strayed to her hair to tuck in an errant curl. Please God, let it be enough, for, if he recognised her, everything would be lost.

'Where is he?' She hated the tight nervousness she was consumed with.

'Over in the corner by the door. He was watching you before. Watching closely.'

Resisting a strong urge to turn around, Emerald summoned up every reserve she had. 'Do you think he suspects?'

'No, for if he did he would have you dragged out of this place immediately, and hanged in the gallows of Tyburn as the daughter of a traitor.'

'He could do that?'

'Oh, you would be surprised what he can do, Emmie, and do with the impunity of a lord who thinks himself so utterly and morally right.'

'Then we must hurry to complete that which we came here to do. Now, look across at him. Slowly,' she added as her aunt's head jolted around. 'Is he carrying a cane of any sort?'

Emerald held her breath as her aunt looked. Could it really be this easy?

'No. He has a drink in his hand. Wine, I think and white.'

She tried not to let her frustration show.

'At least it will not mark this gown.' She had three dresses, procured from the second-hand markets in Monmouth Street, and with a dire lack of funds for any more, did not want this one ruined by a stain that she could never remove.

'Oh, my dear. Surely you do not intend to just bump into him? He would know a sham when he saw one, I am certain of it.'

'Do not worry, Aunt Miriam. I have done this before in Kingston and in Port Antonio when Beau wished for an introduction to some well-heeled stranger. Here it will be easy. Just a small push. Enough at least to allow me the beginnings of a conversation and the chance to be included for a while within his circle of friends.'

'This is the Duke of Carisbrook. Do not underestimate him as your father did.'

Emerald drew in a breath. Beau had become careless but she would not be. Standing, she bent to loosen the silver buckle on her left shoe. The little details needed to be right. She remembered Beau telling her this over and over again.

Asher Wellingham was still speaking with the host when she came in from behind, falling deftly against him. Her small shriek was inspired, she was to think later, for the Duke's reflexes were quick and he had turned to reach for her as she began to lose balance. If the material of her skirt had not caught at the heel of her shoe, she would have been all right. And if the small man beside him had been stronger and kept his feet, all three of them would have stayed upright. But with the highly polished floor and her soft leather soles she could not gain traction and so she simply let herself fall, the splash of wine cold against her skin.

She heard the gasps all around her as the strong arms of the Duke of Carisbrook came under her waist and knees, the black of his superfine jacket soft against her cheek. He was lifting her up against him. Easily.

She felt her own intake of breath at exactly the same moment as she registered the steady beat of his heart, and when his fingers brushed against her bodice, her whole world tilted. Dressed in these ridiculous clothes, the soft swell of her breasts was highly visible and she was taken aback with what she saw in Asher Wellingham's eyes as he carried her from the ballroom. This close, the light brown was webbed with a fine and clear gold and an undeniable masculine interest. For just a second shock disorientated her and everything became immeasurably more difficult.

'You fainted,' he said as he placed her on a sofa in a room away from the dancing. His voice was deep, the finely tuned vowels of privilege easily heard on the edges and his glance held more than a sting of question. With his dark hair slicked back at his nape and his brandy-coloured eyes, the Duke of Carisbrook was unforgettable. A man with legendary confidence and enough gall to pursue her father across three oceans.

And kill him!

Bitter anger congealed with an age-old hurt and, raising the pitch of her voice into something that she hoped resembled embarrassment, she brought her fingers to her mouth.

'I'm utterly and dreadfully sorry,' she gushed, pleased when her sentiment sounded so genuine. 'I think it must have been the heat in the ballroom or perhaps the crush of people. Or the noise, mayhap…' Uncertainly she stopped. Was she overdoing the feminine penchant for histrionics with three excuses all rolled into one? Exaggeration was dangerous, but, dressed in this bone-tight gown and these flimsy, useless shoes, it was also surprisingly easy.

With a quick movement of her fan she hid her eyes

and regrouped her defences, every pore in her body aware of the Duke of Carisbrook, and every problem she now had a direct result of his actions. Swallowing a snaking thread of guilt, she was pleased when he stepped back.

'Was it you who caught me, your Grace?'

'It was more a case of you bouncing off the frail old Earl of Derrick and landing in my arms.'

She tried to look mortified while thinking what hard work it was to be so perpetually sorry, or eternally grateful, and of a sudden the whole charade of being here seemed impossibly more difficult. She didn't belong, couldn't understand the rules or nuances and every instinct told her to be wary. It was anonymity she needed to maintain—if questions were to be asked, they would need answers and she could not give those without endangering everyone she loved. Even the thought made her tremble. 'Where is my aunt?'

'The Countess has gone to find you a shawl for your dress.'

Swinging her legs down off the sofa, Emerald tried to rise. 'If I could stand…'

'I think that it may be wiser to stay still.' His words were husky and her pulse spiked sharply as he placed his finger across the veins of her left wrist. Listening for the beat, she thought weakly, and wondered what he would be making of the pace.

When he smiled she knew. Not a man to incite an insipid reaction from any woman, she determined, not even one as badly turned out as she was. Pulling away her hand, she fanned her face in an exact impersonation of the girls she had watched in many a crowded salon across the past month. 'I am seldom so very clumsy and I cannot think what it was that made me trip…' Lifting the hem of her gown, the loosened silver buckle caught the light. 'It must have been this, I wager…' She let him absorb this and was pleased to see Miriam return, a shawl across her arm and her expression drawn. Lord Henshaw accompanied her.

'Are you feeling better, my dear? You could so easily have knocked your head in the fall and the wine has quite ruined your gown. Here, lean forward and I will wrap this about you.' A bright flame of red-gold material was fastened quickly, although Emerald had had enough of being the wilting centre of attention and stood.

'I will be more careful in future and I thank you for your assistance.' She had to look up at Asher Wellingham as she spoke and, at five foot ten inches in her bare feet, this was not an occurrence that she was often used to. When his eyes caught her own she wished suddenly that her hair was longer and that her gown was of a better quality.

No. No. No.

She shook her head. None of this made sense. Asher Wellingham was her enemy and she would be gone from England as soon as she found what it was she sought. It was the heat in this room that was making her flush and the shock of the fall that had set her heart to pounding. If only she could escape outside and take a breath of fresh air or feel the wind as it made its path along London's river, a hint of freedom on its edge.

Raising her voice to the discordant and high whining tone she had perfected under the tutelage of Miriam, she pushed into her cause.

'I suspect that it was the soles of my shoes that made me falter and the floor itself is highly polished. I do hope that the gossip will not be too unkind.'

'I am certain that it shall not be.' His tone was flat.

'Oh, how very good of you to say so, your Grace,' and although the flare of darkness in his eyes was intimidating she made herself continue. 'Whenever things went wrong at home, Mama always said the strength of a woman's character was not in her successes, but in her failures.'

The tilt of his lips was not encouraging. 'Your mother sounds like a wise woman, Lady Emma.' The sentiment lacked any vestige of interest and she knew that he was fast approaching the end of his patience.

'Oh, she was, your Grace.'

'Was?'

'She died when I was quite young and I was brought up by my father.'

'I see.' He looked for all the world like a man who'd had enough of this discourse, though innate good manners held him still. 'Rumour has it that you are from the country. Which part exactly do you hail from?'

'Knutsford in Cheshire.' She had been there as a child once. It had been summertime and the memory of the flowers of England had never left her. Her mother had pressed one in the locket she now wore. A delphinium, the sky blue dimmed under the onslaught of many years.

'And your accent. I can't quite place it?'

The question startled her and a vase balanced on a plinth near her right hand toppled. A thousand splinters of porcelain fell around her feet. Bending to pick some up, the china pierced through her glove and drew blood.

'Do leave it alone, Emma. This is hardly proper.' Miriam's reprimand was sharp and Emerald froze. Of course, a servant would tidy up after a lady. She must not forget again.

'Is it expensive?' More to the point would she have to pay for it?

Henshaw stepped forward. 'The plinth was shaky and I have never been overly fond of ornate things.'

Wellingham's bark of laughter behind him worried Emerald; looking around, she could also see that this last statement was patently false. Everything in this room was overly embellished and elaborately decorated. Still, given the fact that eighty pounds and a few pieces of jewellery were all that stood between her and bankruptcy, she could hardly afford to be magnanimous.

'I am so terribly sorry.' Desperation stripped her voice to its more familiar and husky tone. She wanted to be away from here. She wanted the wide-open spaces of Jamaica and enough room to move in. She wanted to be safe with Ruby and her aunt and far, far away from a man who could ruin her completely.

But she needed the cane first.

Without the cane, nothing would be possible. Squeezing her eyes together, she was pleased to feel moisture. These Englishmen loved women who were fragile and needy. She had seen this to be true ever since she had arrived here. In the ballrooms. In the drawing rooms. Even in the park where women sat beside their men and watched them tool horses Emerald thought so docile that a child in Jamaica might have managed them. It was just the way of things in England.

She was surprised, therefore, by the Duke of Carisbrook's withdrawal. She had done something wrong, she was sure of it, for his amusement now fled and awkwardness hung between them. Re-evaluating her options, she bit at her lower lip. He was not as the others were here. In looks. In temperament. In size.

Damn it.

Another month and her funds would be spent. Another month and the servants they had hired would be demanding payment and all of London would despise them.

For herself the prospect was not as daunting as the effect such hatred might have on her aunt, for Miriam was old and deserved some comfort in her last years, and her title, although venerable, carried little in the way of income.

Money.

How she hated the fact that it always came back to that. If it had been just her she would have managed, but it wasn't just her anymore. She shivered and pulled the shawl more firmly around her saturated bodice. 'It's cold.' She needed to think, needed to mull over the reaction that the enigmatic Duke seemed to inspire in her, needed to get away and rethink her strategies in this endlessly grey and complex land.

'I will have a footman call up my carriage.' Asher Wellingham was turning even as Miriam stopped him.

'It will not be necessary, your Grace. We are quite able to procure a hackney.'

Emerald, however, having suddenly devised a plan, jumped in.

'We shall be delighted to accept your most generous offer, your Grace, and I trust that the time taken should not inconvenience you.' She glanced at the ornate clock on the mantelpiece. 'Twenty past one, sir. You should have your conveyance back easily before the clock strikes two.'

His shadow dark gaze ran across her. Taking in everything she suspected, and finding her lacking. Face. Manners. Dress. Hair.

'Then I will bid you both good evening.' As she watched him go, she noticed for the first time that he walked with a limp.

The cane, she thought. The cane with the hidden treasure map that Beau swore concealed a fortune. The cane she had come to London for in a last bid to shake off the debtors from her heels and reclaim at least a little of life as it had been.

Doubt passed across her, but she dismissed it. She had to believe in the story Azziz had heard twelve weeks ago in the taverns of Kingston Town. The story that the Duke of Carisbrook had been seen in London using a distinctive carved ebony cane.

Her father's cane, encrusted with emeralds and rubies, the secret catch hidden beneath an overhanging rim of ivory.

Lord, it was all so nebulous, but she had to have faith that it was here, because if it wasn't…? She shook her head. Hard. The alternative didn't bear thinking of and with the covering of darkness the night was still long.

Long enough to waylay a duke?

Her first real chance?

Dressed as a lad, she might be able to shake some clue from Wellingham as to the whereabouts of the map, and if Azziz accompanied her…? Excitement flushed her cheeks as she threaded her hand through her aunt's and helped her from the room. All they needed to know was the location of the cane. With this in hand they could find it and be gone from England on the next outgoing tide. Disappearing was easy when you had the promise of enough money to cover your tracks.

Chapter Two

Two hours later the carriage she had been waiting for thundered out of the Derrick town house, the heavy velour curtains on each side drawn. Signalling to Azziz to urge the team forward and follow, Emerald searched for a place to cut the conveyance off, though as it turned into the docks on the south side of the river, she bade him to hang back.

'What is the Duke doing here at this time of night?'

She asked the question of Toro, who sat beside her, and when he shook his head the ring in his left ear gleamed in the moonlight.

'The tide will be up before morning. Perhaps he means to take ship somewhere.'

Puzzlement was replaced by surprise as a woman she had not seen before climbed down from the now-stationary coach.

No, not a woman, but a girl, she amended, and hardly happy at that. The older man who met with her

had his fingers tightly about her forearm and he wasn't
looking pleased as they walked to the porch of a shabby
doss-house and stopped. Or at least the girl stopped.
Emerald could quite plainly hear her speaking.

'I do not think this is the place we want, Stephen.
You cannot mean to have brought me here.'

'It is just for tonight, Lucy. Just until I can find ship
on the morrow.'

'Nay. You promised we would be wed first.' Her
distress was increasing. 'If my brother found out I
have come to this place…' He did not let her finish.

'I did not force you into the carriage, Lucinda. You
came, I thought, of your own free will. An adventure,
you said, to spice up the boring routine of your existence. Now come along, for we do not have all night.'
His words were slightly slurred.

'Are you drunk?' The young woman's consternation
was becoming more obvious as the driver of the Wellingham coach joined them.

'The master would be most displeased, my lady. My
instructions were to take you straight home.'

'I shall be with you in a moment, Burton. Please,
could you wait in the carriage?'

The servant wavered, plainly uncertain as to what
he should do next and his hesitancy fired the
younger man into an angry response. Without any
warning, his fist shot out and the driver fell dazed
onto the pathway.

'Come, my love, no servant should question a lady's
motives and we have waited long enough for this chance.'

Emerald grimaced. She had heard that tone before and knew what was to come next. A young and inexperienced girl would have no idea how to counter such overt masculine pressure. And would suffer for it.

Breathing out, she pushed forward, signalling to Toro and Azziz to stay behind.

'Let her go.' Her voice was as low and rough as she could make it, the glint of her sharpened blade in the moonlight underlining the message.

'Who the hell are you?'

Ignoring his question, she addressed the girl. 'Think hard and long before you accompany this gentleman, miss, for I think he is not as reputable as you might hope. If I were you, I would take the safer option and return home.'

Emerald tensed as the one named Stephen came towards her and, slipping her blade into the intricate folds of cravat at his neck, she held him still. 'I would advise you, sir, to keep very quiet as to the purpose of this night's excursion. Put it down to folly if you like or to the effects of strong drink, but know that even a small whisper of what has transpired here could be dangerous to your well-being.'

'You would threaten me?'

'Most assuredly I would.'

He moved suddenly, the heel of his hand striking Emerald's cheekbone before she brought the hilt of her knife up hard against the soft part of his temple. He crumpled quite gracefully, she thought, for a tall man and did nothing to cushion his fall. The startled eyes of the girl came upon her and unexpectedly Emerald felt the need to explain away her actions.

'I'd had enough of his questions.'

'So you have killed him?'

'No. Simply wounded his pride. In much the same way as he has wounded yours, I suspect.'

'He was not the person I thought him to be and I can't imagine what may have happened if you had not come along, Mr…?'

'Kingston.' Emerald's heart sank as small, cold fingers entwined around hers.

'Mr Kingston.' The young voice sounded breathless and when Emerald tried to disengage her hand the girl began to cry, tiny sobs at first and then huge loud wrenching ones until the patrons spilled out from a nearby tavern. Emerald was now in a quandary. She was hard-pressed for time and the dawn was not far off and yet she could not just abandon such innocence either.

'How old are you?' she said roughly as she hailed Azziz and waited as he turned the hackney.

'Seventeen. I shall be eighteen, though, in three months and I am indebted to you for your help. If you had not come when you did, I…' Tears rolled down her cheeks and splattered on the yellow silk of her gown.

Oh, dear God, Emerald thought, her own twenty-one years seeming infinitely more worldly. By seventeen she had sailed the world from the Caribbean to the Dutch East Indies, the promise of death dogging her at each and every mile. By seventeen her innocence had long been robbed by circumstance. The thought made her head ache. England was like a hothouse, she suddenly decided, its people so sheltered from reality and difficulty that they were easily hurt. And broken. Like this girl. By small contretemps and silly mistakes.

'If you had not been here…' Lucy began again. 'My brother warned me to have nothing to do with the Earl of Westleigh…said I should stay away from him…insisted that I did not even talk with him.' Her sobs were lessening now and her voice levelled out from panic to anger. 'It was the forbiddenness I think that made him interesting.' She looked down at the man prostrate at her feet. 'Certainly here I can see no re-deeming quality, save for the waistcoat, I think.' She finished on a teary giggle. 'I always liked the way he wore his clothes. By the way, I am Lady Lucinda Well-ingham. The Duke of Carisbrook's youngest sister.'

Emerald stilled a sharp jolt of surprise. Caris-brook's sister? Lord, what was she to do now? The thought that perhaps she could use Asher Welling-ham's sibling as a hostage did cross her mind, but she dismissed this in a moment. For one, she doubted she could stand the company of such a watering pot for any great length of time; for two, she reminded her of a golden retriever they'd had once at St Clair. All gratitude and shining devotion.

No, the girl must be returned post-haste to her brother; if luck held, he might as yet still be at Lord Henshaw's soirée. She could be in and out of the Carisbrook town house without having to speak to a soul, for, damn it, she did not dare to chance any encounter with the Duke. Not dressed like this in the full light of his home.

'Do you know my brother, Mr Kingston? He will be most eager to see that you are compensated for the time and trouble you have taken and I think really that you would like him for he is as practised at the art of fighting as you appear to be and….'

Emerald held up her hand and was glad when the inconsequential chatter finally ground to a halt. She had to think. What was the way of things here? Would it be suspicious to merely drop the girl off at her door? She shook her head and determined that it most probably would be. She would have to play the damn charade out and escort Lady Lucinda home. If Toro drove the coach, he could leave it for the Carisbrook servants to deal with and then rejoin Azziz and her in the hackney.

A compromised solution, but it would have to do. Turning away from the gathering crowd of interested onlookers, Emerald helped the injured driver gain his footing on the carriage steps and was thankful to close the door behind the Wellingham party.

The twelve-hour candle on the library mantelpiece was almost gutted. Another night gone. Relieved, Asher unwound his cravat and threw it on the table. His jacket followed.

Shaking his head, he caught the movement of it in the mirror above his oaken armoire. His eyes were rimmed with darkness.

Darkness.

Frowning, he reached for the brandy, rolling the glass in his hand before swallowing the lot. A quick shot of guilt snaked through him, for he had promised himself yesterday that he would stop drinking alone.

Just another broken vow.

He laughed at the absurdity, though the sound held no humour, and as he settled to what brandy was left in the bottle the image of Lady Emma Seaton in his arms came to mind.

She had smelled nice. Neither perfumed nor powdered. Just clean. Strong. And she had particularly fine eyes. Turquoise, he determined, frowning as the same vague shift of memory he had felt on first seeing her returned.

She was familiar.

But how did he know her? An unusual face. And different. The mark that went through her right eyebrow and up under her fringe was strange. If he were to guess at its origin, he would have placed it as a knife wound. But how could that be? No, far more likely she had been whipped by a branch while riding or tripped perhaps in her youth and caught a sharp edge of stone. He liked the fact that she made no effort to conceal it.

The ring of the doorbell startled him and he checked his watch. Five o'clock in the morning! Surely no acquaintance of his would turn up here at this time and uninvited? Lifting a candle, he strode into the front portico to hear the quiet weeping of his sister.

'My God. Lucy?' He could barely believe it was her as she threw herself into his arms.

'What the hell has happened? Why were you not in the bed you were bound for when you left the Derricks' two hours ago?'

'I…Stephen…met me…in a place…by the port. He said we would be married and instead…'

'Stephen Eaton?'

'He said that he loved me and that if I came to him after the ball tonight he would speak of his feelings. But the place he expected me to accompany him to was hardly proper and then he almost killed Burton…'

'He what…?' Asher made himself simmer down. Redress could come later and calmness would gain him quicker access to answers than rage. 'How did you manage to get home?' He was pleased when his sister did not seem to notice the pure strain of fury that threaded his words.

'A man came with a knife and knocked Eaton out. He put us all in the coach and his driver brought us straight home. A Mr Kingston. He did not know you, for I asked, and his accent was strange.'

'Where is he now?'

'Just gone. He followed us back in a rented hackney and said he would not stay, even though I tried to persuade him differently. He said something of another engagement and promised to send word as to how he could be contacted.'

Asher caught the eyes of his butler and indicated that someone follow the hackney. Blackmail was often a lucrative business and he did not want to be without the facts. Everybody in this world wanted something of him and he could not contemplate this Mr Kingston to be the exception. Still, at least he had brought Lucinda home. And safe. For that alone he would always be grateful.

Gesturing to a maid hovering by the staircase, he bid her take his sister up to bed. He was glad when Lucy went quietly and the sounds of her crying subsided.

It took twenty minutes for Peters to return and the news was surprising.

'The gentleman went to the Countess of Haversham's town lodgings, your Grace. Got out of the hackney and sent it on before disappearing into the house. He had a key, for I tarried to see how he gained entrance. I left Gibbon there to trace his steps further should he surface again.'

'Very good.' Dismissing the messenger, Asher went back into his own study. Emma Seaton and the Countess of Haversham. What did he know of them?

Both niece and aunt were newcomers to London. Miriam had been here for a year and Emma merely a matter of weeks. Both had gowns that had seen better days and the look of women who dealt daily with the worry of dwindling funds, and Miriam kept neither carriage nor horses.

Would they have a boarder living with them as a way of bolstering finances? Or could Emma Seaton have a husband?

And now a further mystery. A young man who would rescue the sister of a very wealthy man and wait for neither recompense nor thanks. A mysterious Samaritan who scurried away from what certainly would have been an honourable deed. In anyone's eyes.

Something wasn't right and in the shadows of wrongness he could feel the vague pull of danger, for nothing made sense. Instinctively his fingers closed hard against the narrow stem of his glass and he sucked in his breath. Harnessing fury. Calculating options.

Emerald pulled the curtain back from her bedroom window on the third floor and cursed. The man was still there and she knew where he had come from.

The Duke of Carisbrook.

He had sent someone after her and she had not bothered to check. Stupid, stupid, stupid mistake, she thought, banging her hand against her sore head and roundly swearing.

She should have sent the conveyance on to some other street and then made her way home undetected. She would have done so in Jamaica, so why not here? With real chagrin she stripped off the boy's clothes and rearranged her blankets beside the bed, glad to lay her head down, glad to close her eyes and think.

What a day. Nothing had gone easily and she did not know the next time she might be in contact with Asher Wellingham.

Close contact.

She remembered the feel of his finger across her

pulse. A small touch of skin that fired her blood. The trick of memory and circumstance, she decided. After all, she had gone to sleep every night for the past five years with those velvet-brown eyes and hard-planed face etched in dream.

The same dream.

The same moment.

The same beginning.

So known now that she could recall each minute detail, even in wakefulness. The sounds, the smell, the sun in her eyes and the wind off the Middle Passage of Turks Island at her back. And a thousand yards of calico luffing in the breeze.

She shook her head hard and made herself concentrate on the sounds of London and on the way the lamp on her side table threw shadows across the ceiling. She would not think of Asher Wellingham. She would not. But desire crept in under her resolution and she flushed as a thin pain entwined itself around her stomach and delved lower.

Lower.

She thought of the bordellos that had dotted the port streets of Kingston Town and wondered. Wondered what it would be like to draw her hands through night-black hair and beneath the fine linen of his shirt. Imaginary sinew and muscle made her pulse quicken and she turned restlessly within the bedclothes, any pressure unwelcome on heated skin.

Her eyes flew open. Lord, what was she thinking? Dread and the cold rush of reality made her shiver.

Asher Wellingham.

Her enemy.

Her father's enemy.

Anger and hurt surfaced and she reached for her wrapper. She would never sleep tonight. Adding another log to the fire, she took a book from the pile beside the chair, 'The Vanity of Human Wishes' in Latin, from Juvenal's satires.

She remembered Beau teaching her the conjugations of complicated verbs from books bound in heavy velvet. Books he had been taught from when he was a child.

A half-smile formed.

Once he had been a patient man. And a good father.

And while she knew he was no angel, he had not deserved the revenge the Duke of Carisbrook had exacted upon him. A calculated retribution timed when the *Mariposa* limped home from a storm in the Gulf of Mexico. Asher Wellingham had come in quickly with three times the manpower and demolished the smaller boat with military precision. Boom-boom, and the masts had gone. Boom-boom, and the front of the brigantine had been holed with a volley of cannon fire.

Azziz had told her the story later when he had been returned to Jamaica on the Baltimore clipper that had picked them out of the sea. The English duke had not given her father the chance to jump, but had demanded a duel on the foredeck of the sinking ship.

And a minute was all it had taken. One minute to run her father through the stomach.

Emerald felt tears prick at the back of her eyes. Her

father had lived by the sword and died by it, but there had been a time when literature and classics and music were more important.

When her mother had been with them! When the family had still been whole. When St Clair had been their home and the *Mariposa* was another man's ship.

Gone. Long gone.

In the depths of longing and promise. And false, false hope.

And it had been a struggle ever since.

With care she replaced the book on the shelf and stood back, distancing herself from the pain of memory, regathering strategies and garnering strength.

Retrieve the cane and return to Jamaica.

Simple plans and the revival of a proper life. Ruby and Miriam and St Clair. Home. The word filled her with longing, even as the amber-fired eyes of Asher Wellingham danced before her. Beguiling. Intriguing. Forbidden.

Shaking her head, she sat down in the chair by the fire and watched the shadows of flame fill the room.

Chapter Three

Asher Wellingham came to Haversham House early the next morning and hard on the heels of a note he had sent. And he came alone.

The drawing room where Miriam and Emerald sat to receive him had been hastily tidied and what little furniture they had in the house had been brought down to fill out the spaces left from an auction they had held almost two months prior in York. Quietly. Secretly. The recompense they had gathered from the exercise had reflected the clandestine nature of the adventure. Still, money could be translated into food and beggars could not be choosers. At least they still had the silver tea service, placed now on a side table.

This morning Emerald wore her second-best gown of light blue velvet with lace trimming around the neckline and an extra petticoat sewn into the base of the wide double skirt for length. On her head she wore a matching mobcap, the scratchy lace making a red rash on the soft underside of her throat. If she had had her potions from home, she might have been able to ease the itchiness. The names on the bottles in the London apothecaries were indecipherable.

Indecipherable!

Everything here seemed that way. Medicines. Places. The weather. People. The Duke of Carisbrook.

'Ladies.' This morning his voice was underlaid with both tiredness and purpose. 'I have come to you this morning on a rather delicate manner.' He cleared his throat and Emerald caught a hint in his eyes of what she could only determine as uncertainty, though the impression was fleeting before the more familiar and implacable urbanity returned. 'I was wondering whether it would be possible to speak with the young man who resides here with you.'

'Young man?' Miriam's response wavered slightly.

'The young man who helped my sister yesterday evening. My servant followed him when he did not stay to be thanked, and it was to this house that he returned. This morning at around the hour of five after sending his carriage on.'

Miriam looked so flabbergasted that Emerald felt bound to break across her silence. 'Perhaps he means Liam, Aunt Miriam?' she prompted and hoped that her aunt might take the hint, though as blankness and silence lengthened she realised she would have to brazen this out by herself. 'Yes, it must be Liam that you speak of. My cousin. He was here for two days only and left this morning for the country, but I shall tell him that you came to relay your thanks. Now,' she added as if the whole subject was decidedly *passé* and she wanted no more discussion, 'would you like tea?'

The Duke's returning glance was so cold that Emerald felt her heart tremble, and his voice when he spoke was fine edged with anger.

'My sister said Mr Kingston had an unusual accent, Lady Emma. Would this accent be the same one as your own?'

'It is, your Grace.' She did not elaborate, but as he swiped his hair back off his face she saw that the two last fingers on his right hand were missing and the stumps where they once had been were criss-crossed in scar tissue.

He has become a ruthless warrior because of the actions of my family.

She made herself stop. She could not feel sorry for a man who had stalked her father and run him through with the sharp edge of his sword. More than once, it was said. And more than what was warranted.

Warranted?

Therein lay the rub. She had heard the story of Asher Wellingham's hatred for her father from every camp except his own. And if life had taught her anything it was the fact that things were seldom black and white. Aye, grey came in many shades. Her father's dreams. Her mother's disappearance. Her own child-hood lost between the scramble for easy gold and the rum-soaked taverns of Kingston Town.

Lord, she had to be careful. She had to appear

exactly who it was she purported to be or else he would know her. Expose her. Consign Ruby to the care of the nuns in the Hill Street Convent for ever. Ruby. Her heart twisted as she remembered the last sight of her little half-sister being bundled away by the dour and formidable Sister Margaret. How long had it been now? Over a hundred days. The time of passage to England and the weeks waiting for Carisbrook to appear. Without the map she could provide neither home nor sustenance, the squalor of the Kingston Town port streets no place for a fey and frightened child of eight.

Accordingly she schooled impatience and, catching the rough gist of her aunt's conversation, observed the man opposite carefully.

This morning he was dressed in fawn trousers and a brown jacket, the cravat matching his white shirt loosely tied in a casual style she had not seen before. With one long leg crossed over the other, he gave the impression of a man well used to power and unquestioned authority and his confidence was contagious after years of living with a father who had little of either.

Damn it, but she must not think like this either. Beau's choices had been foisted on him by his own self-doubt and excessive introspection. If at times he had made decisions that were suspect, he had still tried through it all to provide a home for her and Ruby. A home Asher Wellingham had shattered when he returned to the Caribbean bent on revenge.

Revenge.

His revenge and now her revenge? And what difference lay between them as the thin veneer of right and wrong tumbled under the greater pressure of need? She shook her head and poured the tea. When he stood to take the cup from her, their fingers accidentally met, and everything slowed.

Time.

Breath.

Fear.

The beat of her heart narrowed as she felt the warmth of his skin. Reaching out, she grabbed the arm of the sofa. To stop herself falling. Into him. For ever.

Whatever was wrong with her? She was acting like the simpering misses so prevalent in London and she did not even recognise these constant, damning blushes that seemed to consume her from head to toe. Her resolve firmed.

'Excuse me,' she said when she saw his pupils widen. 'The accident at the ball yesterday has left me rather poorly…' Leaving the explanation in mid-air she noticed that he had placed his cup on the side table as if making ready to catch her again.

Poorly?

When in her life had she ever used such a word? In the fading light of day she suddenly saw herself as he would see her. Vulnerable. Delicate. Feminine. She almost had to repress a smile. So easy to make men believe exactly what you would want them to. So simple to become a person of such little account. Lifting a fan from the table next to her, she was pleased for the cooling breeze it engendered and used the moment to take stock.

Asher Wellingham was older and harder now and the icy brittleness that coated his eyes was disconcerting. Here, in the blandness of a London drawing room, she could feel a barely concealed danger, a thread of the warrior only lightly clothed beneath his well-pressed jacket and pantaloons. Untamed. Ready to pounce should she put a foot wrong. Oh, God, she blanched, she had already put a foot wrong, last night in her haste to get home, and she was worried by the way he watched her now.

How could he not *know me?*

She almost smiled at the whisper of the words as she took a sip of sugary tea, the quick infusion of sweetness bolstering her confidence further. With the practice of one well used to schooling her expression into the shape of something she wasn't, she placed her hand across her mouth and stifled a yawn. Effortlessly.

Asher watched Emma Seaton with an ever-growing feeling of speculation. He could not understand this woman at all. Nothing about her quite made sense. She still wore the same gloves she had had on last night, which was odd given that they were stained. And this morning, although the scar above her eyebrow was still unhidden, a nasty bruise on her cheekbone had been smothered in thick beige face paint in an attempt to conceal it. From whom?

'You have hurt yourself?'

'I fell against the side of a door. Miriam treated it

for me just an hour ago and I hoped it was not too…too noticeable.' Her hand hovered across the mark and he was touched by the movement. She wore the oldest clothes he had ever seen a woman dare to at any social occasion and her hair today was as badly tended as it had been yesterday. Yet she was embarrassed by the bruise upon her face? Nothing about Emma Seaton made sense.

Nothing.

She always wore gloves. She had the same accent as the mysterious and absent Mr Kingston. And she was frightened and decidedly delicate.

Looking around him, other things jarred. The furniture was as badly down at heel as her clothing, yet in the shelf by the window sat well over a hundred books, leather bound and expensive. Kingslake. Wordsworth. Byron and Plato. English was the predominant translation, though many were embellished with the script of the Arabian world. Who the hell here would read those? Defoe stood in company with John Locke, non-conformist authors who chided the establishment with an underlying hint of something darker.

Could the books be Liam Kingston's? He was about to question the Countess on the matter when the doorbell rang and his sister and her maid swept in.

'I am so awfully sorry to just drop in on you like this, Lady Haversham, but I had to come. I am Lady Lucinda Wellingham, and I was informed that Mr Kingston returned home here last night. After he helped me?' The final enquiry was murmured somewhat breathlessly. 'It's just that I would so like to thank him, you see?'

Asher crossed the room to stand by his sister. 'Liam Kingston has departed, Lucinda. Back to…?' His voice was filled with question.

'His home.' Miriam's hesitation shrieked volumes.

'But he will return?' Lucy could barely contain her interest.

'I do not think so. No.' Emerald had regained her wits now that Lucy Wellingham's face held not even the slightest hint of recognition. 'He is married, you see, and his wife is from America. From Boston. She wants to move back there as soon as she has had her fourth child.'

Lucinda paled noticeably. 'Married with four children?' She gawped. 'But he hardly looked old enough.'

'Oh, people are always saying that to him. Are they not, Aunt?' Desperation lent her voice credence and she was pleased to see Miriam nod vigorously. 'Perhaps in the dark you did not see him properly.'

The Duke of Carisbrook's face was inscrutable, though his sister insisted on some recompense. 'We are going to Falder next week, Asher. Could we not invite the Countess and her niece? As a means of saying thank you.'

Emerald's heartbeat accelerated at the question.

'Indeed.' His reply could hardly have held less of a welcome, but, seeing the glimmer of opportunity, she seized upon it.

'We would be delighted to visit your home, Lady Lucinda. Why, I could hardly think of anywhere I should rather go.'

A way into Falder. A first unexpected providence. And although Emerald wished that he could have shown more enthusiasm for the promise of their company, she was not daunted. One night. That was all it would take.

'And your cousin, Liam Kingston, would be most welcome,' Lucinda added, 'for I should deem it an honour to thank him for his assistance in person.' She gripped her brother's arm in entreaty and Asher Wellingham inclined his head in response.

'Bring him along by all means, Lady Emma, for a man who can dispose so summarily of the Earl of Westleigh and deliver my sister home without recompense is to be much admired.'

The thought did cross Emerald's mind that his voice had an odd edge of question to it but she couldn't be certain, for he did not look at her again before gathering his sister's hand into his own and politely bidding them goodbye.

As they heard his carriage pull away, Miriam began to smile. 'I would say that went very well, would you not, my dear? Aye, very well indeed.'

Emerald crossed to the window and looked out.

Very well?

She wondered if her aunt needed new glasses and smiled at the thought before gingerly touching her own throbbing cheekbone.

* * *

'What do you know about the Countess of Haversham, Jack?' Asher leaned back in a chair in his library and drew on his cigar. He'd barely managed an hour of sleep last night but, with his body mellow with brandy, the peace here was pleasant. For just a moment the familiar anger that haunted him was quieter.

'Her husband, Matthew, died from heart failure five years back and it was said that his gambling debts were substantial.'

'So the Countess sold off the furniture to pay her creditors?'

'She what?'

'Sold off the furniture. I was at the Haversham town house in Park Street this morning and there were three chairs and a table in one room and little else in any of the others.'

Jack leant forward, intrigued. 'That explains the gowns they wear then. And the niece's hairstyle. Home-done, I would wager, and by her very own hand, though there was something Tony Formison told me yesterday that did not ring true. He said that Lady Emma had not come down from the country at all, but had arrived a few months ago aboard one of his father's ships with two black servants and a number of very heavy-looking chests.'

Asher began to laugh. The books he had seen in the drawing room? They were hers? 'Formison was on the docks when she arrived?'

'Aye, and he said that he could have sworn her hair was longer.'

'Longer?'

'To her waist according to Tony, and looking nothing like it appears to now.' He stood and retrieved his hat from the table beside him, bending to look at the label on the bottle as he did so. 'It's late and long past the time that I should have been home, but you always have such fine brandy, Asher. Where's this one from?'

'From the Charente in France.'

'A boon from your last trip?'

Asher nodded. 'I'll have some sent to you, but in return I want you to find out from Formison exactly where the boat that brought Emma Seaton to London came in from. Which port and which month.'

Jack's eyebrows shot up.

'Ask discreetly and in the name of precaution, for I don't want problems resulting from this information.'

'Problems for Emma Seaton or problems for yourself? I thought you seemed rather taken by her at my ball.'

'You misinterpret things, Jack. I put my arms out and caught her as she threw herself against me. Hard, I might add, and with none of the wiles that I am more used to. Before she had even hit the floor she had her eyes open; there was a calculation there that might be construed as unnerving.'

Jack began to laugh. 'You're saying she may have done it on purpose?'

'I doubt I'll ever know, though a betting man would have to say that the odds were more than even.' The humour faded quickly from his eyes as he continued. 'Besides, I am too old to fall for the tricks of a green and simpering country miss.'

'You're thirty-one and hardly over the hill and Lady Emma is…different from the others…less readable. If you are not interested in her, then I sure as hell am.'

'No!' Asher was as surprised by the emotion in the word as Jack was, and to hide it he collected the remains of the brandy and corked the top. 'For the road,' he muttered as he handed the bottle to him, swearing quietly as the door shut behind his departing friend.

Emma Seaton.

Who exactly was she? For the first time in a very long while a sense of interest welled to banish the ennui that had overcome him after Melanie's death.

Melanie.

His wife.

He fingered the ring that he wore on his little finger, the sapphires wrought in gold the exact shade of eyes he would never see again. Her wedding ring. His glance automatically went to the missing digits of his other hand. With good came bad.

He frowned and remembered his return to England after a good fourteen months of captivity. Any innocence he might have been left with had been easily stripped away. He was different. Harder. He could see it reflected in the face of his brother and in the eyes of his mother and aunt. Even his impetuous·sister was afraid, sometimes, of him.

Running his hand through his hair, he frowned.

Brandy made him introspective. And Emma Seaton touched him in places that he had long thought of as dead.

It was the look in her eyes, he decided, and the husky timbre of her voice when she forgot the higher whine. She gave the impression of a frail and fragile woman, yet when she had fallen against him at the ball he had felt an athletic and toned strength. The sort of strength that only came with exercise or hard work.

He was certain that the mishap had been deliberate and he tried to remember who else had been standing beside him. Lance Armitage and Jack's father John Derrick, older men with years of responsibility and solid morality behind them. Nay, it was him she had targeted and now he had asked her to Falder.

On cue?

No, that could not possibly be. He was seeing problems where none existed. The woman was scared of her own shadow, for God's sake, and unusually clumsy. She was also threadbare poor. A wilder thought surfaced. Was she after the Carisbrook fortune? A gold digger with a new and novel way of bagging her quarry? He remembered the countless women who had tried to snare him since Melanie's death.

Lord, he thought and lifted a candlestick from the mantelpiece before opening the door and striking out for the music room. Melanie's piano stood in a raft of moonlight, the black and white keys strangely juxtaposed between shadows. Leaning against the mahogany, he pressed a single note and it sounded out against the silence, a mellow echo of vibration lost in darkness.

Like he was lost, he thought suddenly, before dismissing the notion altogether. He was the head of the Carisbrook family and everybody depended on him. If he faltered…? No, he could not even think of the notion of faltering. Carefully he replaced the lid of the piano across the keys. Dust had collected upon the hinges and had bedded into the intricate inlaid walnut that spelled out his wife's initials.

Ash unto ash, dust unto dust.

Tomorrow he would inform his housekeeper to instruct the staff to clean the music room again. It had been too long since he had forbidden its use to anyone save himself. And his wife would have abhorred the fact that her prized piano had sat unplayed for all these years.

Still, he could not quite leave the room, an essence of something elusive on the very edges of his logic.

Something to do with Emma Seaton. Her turquoise eyes. The scar. The sound of laughter against the sea.

The sea?

Was he going mad? He crossed to the window. Outside the night was still. Dark. Cold. And the cloud that covered the moon made his leg ache, shattered bone healed badly into fragments.

Fragments.

They were all that was left of him sometimes, a shaky mosaic of loss and regret.

'God,' he whispered into the night. 'I am becoming as maudlin as my mother.' Blowing out the candle, he resolved to find some solace in his library. At least till the dawn when he could sleep.

* * *

Azziz returned to the house in Park Street just before midnight, and Emerald hoped that this time he had been careful to scour the neighbouring roads to make certain he was unobserved.

'I have heard word on the docks that McIlverray is on his way to London, Emmie.'

'Then he knows about the cane—why else would he come?' She frowned; this news put a whole different perspective on everything. Karl McIlverray, her father's first mate, was as corrupt as he was clever and had a band of loyal men who followed him blindly. Any intelligence circulating the docks of Kingston Town usually ended up in his ears and Karl McIlverray had been with her father long enough to put two and two together. He would know exactly what was inside the cane.

Damn, it was getting more and more complicated and she wished for the thousandth time that her father had kept the treasure in the vault of a bank or in a safe where it could have been more easily accessed.

Time. It was slipping away from her.

How long before he arrives?'

'A week or even ten days—the storms out in the Atlantic might slow them down, if we are lucky. I'll leave a man in place to make certain we see them before they see us.'

'And you?'

'Toro and I will come to Falder. We can camp somewhere close and keep an eye on things.'

Emerald was not certain as to the merits of the plan for they would be easily seen in the English countryside around the house. But if McIlverray came, she would need to be able to summon help, and quickly. She imagined the aristocratic Carisbrook family coming face to face with any of them and her heart pounded. And if someone innocent got hurt because of her…! She could not finish.

She had to be in and out of Falder quickly and on a boat back to Jamaica, making sure in the interim that Karl McIlverray had word of her movements. Another more worrying thought occurred to her.

'What if the cane is back here in London?'

Azziz frowned. 'It wasn't in the house a month ago when Toro and I searched it.'

'But he may have brought it with him this time. The limp still troubles him.'

'Have you seen him use a cane at all in public?'

'No.' She began to smile. 'And I do not think that he would. Each time I have been in his company he is careful that others may not notice the ailment. A cane would only draw their attention to what he seeks to hide.'

Privacy. Sanctuary. She sensed these things were important to the enigmatic Duke of Carisbrook and her spirits lifted.

'Miriam and I are due to leave for Falder soon and I can search the house easily under the cover of night.'

'The Duke of Carisbrook does not strike me as a man who could be easily fooled.'

'How does he strike you then?'

'Tough. Dangerous. Ruthless. A man who would have little time for lies.'

'Then I must be out of Falder before he knows them as such.'

'Do not underestimate him, Emmie.'

'You are beginning to sound like Miriam.' She smiled and laid her hand on his arm, her fingers tightening as she remembered all the other times in her life she had depended on Azziz. If she lost him too…? If anything went terribly wrong…? As she tried to banish fear she was consumed by sadness. When was the last time that she had taken a breath in joy and let all of it out again?

She could barely remember.

Her father's death, Miriam's agedness, and a debt that was increasing with each and every passing day. She could go neither backwards nor forwards and the options of anything else were fast shrinking. What happened to people who ran out of money in London? She shook her head in fright.

The poorhouse took them.

The place of liars and cheats.

A liar. It was who she had become. If she could find the map, she could fashion a home. Not a grand one, but a for-ever place. A place to stay and grow and be. A place like St Clair. She closed her eyes against the pure thread of desperation that snaked itself around her heart, because she knew that the old house was gone, up in flames, the living embodiment of the McIlverray hatred for her father. And grounded perhaps on a sense of justice, for Beau had promised Karl McIlverray far more than he had ever delivered.

She let out her breath. Beau had promised everyone more than he had ever delivered and she needed to make it right.

Right?

If she hadn't been so worried, she might have smiled at the thought. Right? Wrong? Good? Bad? She remembered Beau's interpretation of law and doubted that Asher Wellingham's would be even remotely similar. Enormous wealth and righteous morals were easy when you were not staring down the barrel of a gun and saying what you thought the bearer would most like to hear.

Lies and deception.

It was all that she was left with as truth withered under the harsher face of reality.

Azziz pulled his blade from the leather sheath at his shin and wiped it with an oiled rag from his pocket. The movement caught her attention.

The sheer danger of it all was no longer as exhilarating as it had once been. Now, instead of seeing the adventure in everything she saw the pitfalls, and an encounter with McIlverray worried her a lot more than she allowed Azziz to see that it did.

Was she growing old?

Twenty-one…twenty-two in six months. Sometimes now she caught herself looking across at other women her age as they walked the streets with husbands and children at their side.

She tried to remember what her own mother had looked like, tried to remember the touch of her hand or the cadence of her voice and came up with nothing.

Nothing. The emptiness of memory caught at her with a surprising melancholy. To distract herself, she began to speak of the entertainment for the following night.

'There is a party at the Bishop of Kingseat's that I am indebted to attend. Lady Flora has been generous in her friendship…' She faltered.

'Will Carisbrook be there?'

'I think so.'

'Miriam said he seemed interested in you. If he should find out even a little—'

'I know,' she interrupted Azziz before he went further and was glad when he left the room for the kitchens on the ground floor to find his supper.

Chapter Four

At a gathering at the home of the Bishop of Kingseat the following evening, Asher again met Emma Seaton. The result, he suspected, of their encounter at Jack's ball and the host's wife's penchant for matchmaking. If he had liked the Learys less he might have left on some simple pretence, but George had been a good friend to his father and Flora was a woman of uncommon sensitivity.

Today, as Flora Leary turned to attend to a question another guest had asked of her, Emma Seaton looked rather nervous. Asher saw that the lace on the top of one of her gloves had been badly mended and that the gown she wore was at least a size too big. The colour was odd too. Off-brown and faded in patches. None of this seemed to faze her, though, and her confidence in a room full of well-dressed ladies was endearing. The bruise on her cheek was barely visible today.

'Lady Emma. You look well.'

'Thank you, your Grace.' Folding down the sleeve of her gown to cover the torn lace, she took a sip of the orgeat she was drinking. 'I was certain that Lady Flora had mentioned just a small gathering?'

He looked up. Only forty or fifty people milled around the salon.

'At Falder a little supper would constitute thrice this number,' he remarked and she coloured. But it was not embarrassment that he saw in her eyes when she met his glance, but irritation.

Sea blue.

Her eyes were turquoise and outlined with a clear sea blue. Here in the light it was easy to see today that which he had missed yesterday.

'My family was a quiet and modest one. My father was religious, you see. Very religious. And time spent in the company of others was time that he could not spend in prayer.'

'A devout man, then?'

She nodded and fiddled with the fan she held. 'With an equally devout family.'

'You are Catholic?'

'Pardon?'

'Catholic? The persuasion of your beliefs?'

'Oh, indeed.'

'And which church do you attend in London?'

The fan dropped out of her hands and onto the floor, surprising them both. As he leaned down to fetch it for her, she did the same and her bodice dipped in the middle. *She wore nothing beneath.* No stays. No chemise.

No bindings. Two beautifully formed breasts topped with rosy nipples fell into his sight and were gone again as she righted herself.

He felt his body jolt in a way he had not felt for years and shifted his position to better accommodate the hardening between his thighs. God, he was at the house of a bishop and the woman next to him was completely naked under her ill-fitting dress. He could barely believe it. Heat and lust made the cravat he wore feel tight and he was annoyed when Charlotte Withers, a woman whose company he had once enjoyed, came over to him.

'It has been an age, your Grace, since I have seen you in London. I had heard that you were here and I suppose on reflection you were down for Henshaws' ball. The evening before last, was it not, and all the gossip of how the Duke of Carisbrook was cajoled into falling for the wiles of a green and fainting country miss.'

'Not a faint, but a fall,' he returned and moved forward, pleased to see a blush mark Charlotte's cheeks when she saw who stood next to him.

'Lady Emma! I did not realise you were here and I apologise for any hurt you may have suffered from my careless remarks. Are you quite recovered from your mishap?'

'I am and I thank you for your concern.' Emma Seaton's reply contained no little amount of irony.

'Your accent eludes me,' Charlotte remarked as she recovered her equilibrium. 'Where exactly are you from?'

'My mother was French.'

Asher frowned. She had answered another question without telling anyone anything.

'So it is your father who is related to the Countess of Haversham?

'Was. He died last year from the influenza. A wicked case it was, too, according to the doctor; it took him a long time to succumb to the effects of the infection. One moment hot and the next cold. Why, I pray nightly to the Lord above that I should not see another soul die in such a way.'

'Yes. Quite.' Charlotte looked away to the riper pickings of Percy Davies who had come to her other side and Asher, while silently applauding Emma Seaton's skilful evasion, decided to up the stakes a little.

'Charlotte Withers is a notorious gossip and an in-veterate meddler. If you were to entrust any secrets to her I am certain that they should be all over town by the morning.'

As the colour drained out of Emerald's cheeks, the smile he gave her was guarded.

Could he be warning her? For just a second she wanted to fold her fingers around his and pretend that he offered protection. Here. In London, where each battle was carried out with words and sly innuendos. Where the people said one thing and meant another. She didn't understand them. That was the trouble. She had come to England woefully unprepared and desper-ately different. It showed in her accent, in her clothes, in the way she walked and moved and sat.

Pity.

She had seen it written all over his handsome face as his glance had brushed over the torn lace on her glove and the generous fitting of her gown. Pity for a woman who, when compared with the other refined beauties, personified by the likes of Lady Charlotte, fared very badly. Gathering her scattered wits, she tried to regroup.

'Secrets?'

'My sources say you arrived in England not from the country, but from Jamaica?'

She laughed, congratulating herself on the inconsequential and tinkling sound. 'And they would be right. I came back to England after sorting out my father's possessions when he died, and setting his affairs into order.'

'Your father was a scholar?'

A scholar? Oh God, what was he referring to now? And just who were his sources? She was pleased when Lord Henshaw caught her attention.

'Lady Emma. Are you feeling better?'

'Yes. Very much better, thank you.' Such a polite society, Emerald thought, as she gave him her answer. Such a lot unsaid beneath every question. She pulled her fingers away and laid her hands against the voluminous skirt of her gown.

'Did you hear of Stephen Eaton's problem the other night, Asher? He met with footpads by the dockside and has a wicked lump on his head. The local constabulary are out in force to try to find the culprits. Word is that it's a shocking state of affairs when a gentleman cannot even ride around London without being robbed and beaten.'

'He is saying he was robbed?'

'Yes, though I cannot work out for the life of me what he was doing at that time and in that part of London, given he had left my ball only an hour or so earlier. His watch and pistol were taken and a ring he wore upon his hand that was a family heirloom. Diamonds, I think. He plans to spend the next few months abroad to recover from the assault, his mother says. I saw her this morning.'

'A fine scheme. I hope he takes his time to make a full recuperation. If you see his parents, do acquaint them with my sentiments, and say that I was asking after him.' Pure steel coated his words.

'I will do just that. Does your sister know of his mishap?'

'My sister?'

'Lucinda. She has danced with him at several parties and I thought perhaps there was a special friendship...'

Jack's voice tailed off. Emerald was certain that he had just put it all together and also deduced that this was neither the time nor the place to discuss such things. She saw him chance a quick look at Charlotte Withers behind him before he changed the subject entirely.

'My oldest sister was hoping to visit Annabelle Graveson next month, Asher. How is she keeping.'

'Very well.' His tone was amused as he finished off his drink. 'You will meet the Gravesons this weekend at Falder, Lady Emma.'

'Are they relatives, your Grace?'

'No. Annabelle Graveson was married to my

father's friend. When he died, he asked me to watch over the affairs of his wife and son.'

Jack Henshaw joined in the conversation. 'The old Duke was a philanthropist and Asher has inherited his own bevy of needy folk.'

Asher said nothing, but Emerald could tell that he was not happy at his friend's summation of duty. Interesting, she thought, for a man who professed to caring for little as he held the world at bay.

Looking around, she noticed an attractive dark-haired woman whose eyes were fastened on the Duke of Carisbrook, but if he felt her regard he gave no indication of it as he leant towards her as if to shelter his words from the others around them.

'Eaton is using the ploy of a robbery to ease his guilt, I would suspect. Though there is another explanation. How honest is your cousin?'

'As honest as I am, for the ten commandments were the bread and butter of our childhood.' She felt the distinct turn of guilt in her stomach.

'You never lie?'

'My father taught us the importance of truth and honesty.'

She forced back conscience and stiffened when he reached for the locket dangling on a long chain about her neck.

'Is this some family crest?'

'My mother's,' she replied softly and deposited the golden trinket down again between her breasts, glad when he did not pursue the topic.

'Who was French?'

She looked at him blankly. 'Pardon.'

'You said that your mother was from France.' He was so close she could have reached out a finger to run along the hard cut of his jaw.

'I did? Yes, of course I did. Because she was.' Lord, this lying was eating at her composure and she felt sweat in the palms of her hands.

'*Êtes-vous originaire du sud ou bien du nord de la France?*'

What was it he had said? Something of north and south. This much she had translated, though the other was lost to her.

'*Oui.*' She chanced one of the ten or so French words she actually knew and was disconcerted by the amusement scrawled on his face.

'And honesty was as important to your mother as it is to you?'

'Yes, your Grace.'

'Admirable,' he returned and as his eyes glanced across the loose material of her gown she felt the skin on her nipples pucker and folded her arms. She should have worn her underclothing, but it felt so much better without it.

'It is seldom one meets a woman of such high moral fibre.'

The blood rushed into her face. 'I will take that as a compliment, your Grace,' she said simply.

His laughter brought the conversation around them to a noticeable quietening and as she looked up the hostess, Lady Flora, caught her eye and smiled broadly. Emerald observed that the green-eyed beauty standing next to their host didn't look anywhere near as friendly as she posed a question.

'I hear that your newest ship is ready for a launch here in London, your Grace. What is it to be called?'

'The *Melanie*.'

An inexplicable tension filled the room.

Who was Melanie, she wondered, and what was she to Asher Wellingham? Someone important, no doubt. Someone he loved?

But where was she now?

The Bishop of Kingseat raised his glass.

'To the *Melanie,* then. May she ride the waves long and true and be as beautiful as her namesake.'

There it was again. Her namesake? Interest flared as Asher acknowledged the toast and drank and Emerald was struck by the difference five years had made in the lines of his face.

Hardness and distance.

For some reason the thought made her unfathomably sad and when the topic turned to dancing she was pleased, for it gave her time to compose herself.

Half an hour Emerald stood alone near a pillar that led off to a balcony. Asher Wellingham was across the other side of the room with the beautiful green-eyed woman draped across his arm. From this distance the darkness of her carefully coiffed hair was exactly the same shade as his. The memory of her own hair was sharp and she raised her hand to pat down the short errant curls.

Two ladies behind her were talking about the Duke and she turned so that she could overhear them more easily.

'If only he would look our way, Claire. Just once. Would it be considered rude, do you think, to raise one's glass and smile at him?'

The other girl began to laugh. 'Oh, you would never do that, surely. Imagine what he might think of us.'

'It is rumoured that he will go to India next month. Let us hope that he does not meet the ghost of the pirate Beau Sandford on his travels.'

A loud squawk of titillation brought the Duke's glance their way, and Emerald tensed. Hearing the name of her father here disorientated her because it was so very unexpected. Her heartbeat accelerated when she saw the subject of the girl's conversation start towards her.

'Lady Emma? Would you walk with me for a moment?'

'Walk with you?' Her astonishment was such that she forgot to use her carefully perfected girly voice.

'There is a balcony just here overlooking a garden. I thought it a good place to talk and I have something for you.'

More of an order than a request. She ignored the arm he held out and hoped that he had not seen the imprinted adulation on the faces of the young women around her. His arrogance was already legendary enough.

The balcony was open at one end and she welcomed the quietness of it. A group of other people stood near the French doors that led in from the main room; pausing by the railing she waited for him to speak.

'Lucy gave me something to give to you and I had my man return home for the letter when I saw that you were here tonight.' He dragged a sealed envelope out of his pocket. 'It is for your cousin, Liam Kingston. A letter of thanks, I should imagine but Lucinda is young and impressionable, so if the correspondence seems exaggerated in places—' He stopped as she held out her hand and his fingers inadvertently touched her own. She shivered. Even here in the most public of places and with the simplest of contacts she was vulnerable. Hoping that her face did not hold the same expression as the vacuous women inside, she tucked the letter unread into her reticule.

'If Mr Kingston could find it in him to send a reply and state his circumstances, I would be grateful. Seventeen-year-old girls have a propensity for imagination, you understand, and I would like the matter resolved.'

There it was again. Responsibility and control. Important to a man like Asher Wellingham and something he rarely let go of.

What would happen if he did let go of it? a small voice questioned. As the blood hammered in her temples she turned away to give herself a moment to recover and his next words came through a haze.

'Would it be possible for you to give me his direction? When I am next in his part of the world I could call in on him and give my thanks.'

Lord!

What address could she tell him? She knew no one in the Americas. A happier thought surfaced. Perhaps Azziz had contacts…

'I will write it down for you and have it delivered.'

He shook his head. 'You will be in Falder in two days. I can wait until then.'

The strain of the supper waltz rent the air.

'How is it that I know you, Lady Emma? Have we met before?'

'Are you familiar with Cheshire, your Grace?' She was relieved when he smiled at her question and shook his head.

'No, but I do not think the memory of you lingers from England somehow…'

Desperate to take his mind from recollection, she locked her hand on his and asked him to dance, completely ignoring the look of astonishment on his face.

His body melded against her own and found the rhythm of the music with much more finesse than she did. Leaning into him for just a moment she closed her eyes.

Wishing.

Wishing that she was a well-born lady and that he might like her just a little. Wishing that things could have been different between them and that all he believed of her was true.

Asher felt her relax against him and pulled her closer. He had not asked anyone to dance with him since Melanie.

In truth, he had not asked Emma Seaton to dance with him either and yet here she was, the warm whisper of her breath tantalising in the folds of his neck. Close. Unexpected. Had she not listened to gossip?

A quick glance at the interest on the faces of others made him wary and he pulled back, the distance between them wider now.

'You are new to town, Lady Emma. If you want your reputation to stay intact, it might be as well to avoid me as your supper partner.'

'And why would that be, your Grace? The girls who stood behind me inside would have liked an introduction and they looked innocuous enough.'

He began to laugh. 'Where were you schooled?'

She was taken aback. 'In a convent. Why?'

'Because your vocabulary is…surprising.' Emerald sensed a new emotion in him that was difficult to interpret. 'Have you had any offers yet?'

'Offers?'

'Of marriage. Isn't that why you have come to London?'

The blood drained out of her face.

'You did not know this to be the Season? The time for men to choose from the year's débutantes.'

'Men like you?' she countered and tried to sound indifferent.

'If you had been listening to the gossip, you would

know that the state of holy matrimony is something that I have become adept at avoiding.'

'Oh. I see.' The uneasy sensation of being played for a fool suddenly overcame her. 'Then you will be pleased to know that I am not on the look out for a husband either, your Grace.'

'Really.' His brows raised. 'What are you here for then, Lady Emma?'

Two things hit Emerald simultaneously. The lazy devastation of his smile and the husky timbre of his voice. Her spine tingled with an odd and lonely pain as she remembered a younger Asher Wellingham standing on the transom of his ship, eyes blazing under the emotion of a high-seas' battle and releasing her from the sharp tip of his sword only when he determined her not to be the lad he thought she was, but a girl. And now here in the ballroom of a beautiful English house she understood what she had only half-known then.

The Duke of Carisbrook was an honourable man and one who respected the codes of England's aristocracy. Gentlemen did not hurt women. Even ones who could wield a weapon with as much finesse as any man aboard the *Mariposa*.

'I am here to see to the welfare of my aunt. She is old and lonely and I am the very last of her family.'

'And very deaf?'

'Pardon?'

'Deaf. Hard of hearing. A woman who would sleep through the night no matter what might happen in her house.' A glint in his eyes softened the insult. 'Your cousin, Liam Kingston, for instance, keeps hours that a poor sleeper might find tiring.'

Despite everything she laughed. 'And for your sister's sake it is just as well that he does.'

'Indeed,' he returned. 'A lucky coincidence that. What was your cousin doing following the Carisbrook coach in the first place?'

'Pardon?'

'My driver noticed a carriage dogging his heels through the city streets. On memory he would say it to be a hired hack and I know that your aunt does not keep a conveyance.'

She was silent. Lord, he had worked it all out with little more than a passing clue.

'Perhaps he was mistaken. Liam has only recently come to London and I can think of no reason for him to be following your sister.'

'Can you not? Then perhaps it was me he wanted.'

'And what would my cousin want with you?'

'That's the same question I have been asking myself these past few days.' His voice was laconic.

'And did you find an answer, your Grace?'

'I did not, Lady Emma.'

Leaning back, the lights glinted off his timepiece and threw refracted rainbows across the floor at his feet. Danger and stealth. And manners. Was there ever a combination quite so appealing?

'My cousin is a wealthy and respectable married man.'

'So you say.'

'Who makes his money from cotton,' she continued, not liking the disbelief she could so plainly hear in his voice. 'He would have no need for blackmail, if that is what you are suggesting.'

'I suggested nothing.'

'Or kidnapping,' she continued and then bit down on her lip. Lord, she was being drawn into showing her cards by a master. The thought had her temper rising. Dredging up every skill she had ever shown in acting, she plastered a smile on her face.

'Why, your Grace, it is really too bad of you to jest me, for surely that is what all this is.'

'Assuredly,' he returned, bowing as the music stopped, implacable politeness replacing the humour. 'Although sometimes I greatly doubt that you are quite as vapid as you make out to be.'

Emerald's heartbeat faltered at the tone and without even trying she could see the lonely mantle of distance that lay between him and everyone, keeping them back and away.

Cross this line and be damned.

The missing fingers and his limp underplayed the jeopardy, but she could not afford to let her guard down.

Supper had been set up on a long table to one end of the salon, and Asher led her over to join the Learys and Jack Henshaw and Charlotte Withers at one of the smaller tables around it. After finding them each a plate of food, he sat down beside her and the topic turned to music.

'Do you have a speciality, Lady Emma? An instrument that you play.' Flora Leary's eyes were full of interest.

'No. I am afraid not.' She did not imagine that the harmonica was the sort of instrument the Bishop's wife would be thinking about.

'Can you sing?'

'No.' God forbid that she should have to stand in front of this crowd and croon a bawdy number learnt at the knees of sailors who had never so much as graced a salon even a quarter as reputable as this one. 'My father was a man who believed music to be a facet of the Devil's mind. A religious man, you understand, of strong beliefs and an utter conviction in the rightness of them.'

'Not an easy man to live with, then.' Asher joined in the conversation and an undercurrent threaded his words. 'What is it that you are well versed in?'

Emerald struggled to think up accomplishments that would be acceptable to this company. 'I am a proficient rider and excellent in the preparation of meals.'

The heavy silence around the table lengthened as she realised the extent of her mistake.

'Surely you mean the planning of menus, Lady Emma? A most salutatory undertaking. Why, I remember my mother enjoyed the art of putting together meat and wine. It quite took up much of her time before a grand meal. Was it that sort of thing you meant, my dear?' The kind and gracious Lady Flora gave her an easy way out and she gladly took it.

'Yes. Just exactly that.'

Lady Charlotte leaned forward and laid her fingers along the line of Asher Wellingham's arm. 'Your brother Taris was always a connoisseur of fine wines, your Grace. How is he? Has his sight improved?'

'Markedly.'

'Well, that is the most pleasing news I have heard in a while. Tell him I was asking after him, and if he is down in London in the near future…'

'I will.'

Emerald felt that something was not quite as it should be. She knew that Taris was Asher's brother, for Miriam had given her a vague outline of his immediate family. But the fact that he had some problem with his sight had not been mentioned at all and the mask that shuttered any trace of emotion on the Duke of Carisbrook's face was intriguing.

A brother with a sight problem and a woman named Melanie who, apart from being beautiful, was also absent from his life. He had many secrets and held every emotion beneath a rigid self-control.

Discipline and governance had etched a hard line between his eyes, puncturing a face of pure masculine beauty into something less easy—whenever she was near him she felt a pull of sadness, the world stretched out of shape. Even here in the bland world of London society he did not relax as the others did, but looked around.

A constant check on safety.

She was certain that if someone had come up unexpectedly behind him he would have used the small knife hidden in the folds of his jacket. And used it well. She smiled. It was intriguing, this mix of mannerisms. The crest of ducal importance counterpoised by a dangerous fighting ability.

She had seen it, after all, and knew what he was capable of. Knew too that these people who fawned over his title and wealth had absolutely no idea: the wash of blood and guts across the deck on the high seas and the wailing agony of hurt.

Her life.

His life for a time.

For the time it had taken her to extinguish honour and send him hurtling downwards into the boiling anger of the ocean.

Asher instructed his driver to go fast through the dark London streets and, opening a window, enjoyed the breeze on his face and the sky above his head. Dotted with stars tonight, he mused. A small respite in a month of rain. His brother would be pleased, for watching the heavens through the telescope he had had shipped over especially from China was a passion he could still enjoy. He grimaced. But for how long?

Taris's sight was worse. He admitted it to himself and cursed Charlotte Withers for asking. Emma Seaton would be at Falder the day after tomorrow and he did not want her to know the extent of the problem.

He wanted no one to know.

He wanted to keep the world away from his brother until he could fashion a solution. Until he knew for certain what it was they were facing. Total loss of sight? Partial vision?

If only Taris had not come out to the Caribbean to find him after the ransom note had been sent. If only he had stayed here in England and left the danger of rescue to others. No, he could not think like that. Taris had come and he had been saved. The high price of his brother's sacrifice paid ever since with his own crippling guilt over his brother's blindness.

'God, help me,' he whispered to a deity that tonight felt close, though the vision of Emma Seaton's lack of underclothing juxtaposed strangely against his request, and for a second amusement filled the more familiar void of loneliness.

Her soft skin on her right breast had been marked with an indigo tattoo. A butterfly. Tiny. Delicate. Unexpected.

Curiosity welled. An emotion he had not felt in years. It was a relief to laugh. Even to himself out here in the night.

Emma Seaton.

Her hair was curly when it was loosened from the pins that tightly bound it. Stray tendrils had worked themselves free at her nape and the ringlets that hung only to her collar were tightly coiled. Red-blonde hair and turquoise eyes. And a body well endowed with the curves of womanhood.

He shook his head and rubbed at the stiff muscles on the back of his neck. He had enjoyed tonight. Enjoyed her humour and her candidness. Enjoyed the view of sun-warmed skin that lay beneath her loose bodice and the feel of her in his arms as they had danced.

What would she look like in silks and satins and with her hair dressed by the best of London's hair salons?

He swore roundly. He had seldom kept a mistress in the way other men of the *ton* did. Oh, granted he had occasionally used the services of select women who could be relied on for their discretion, yet tonight, with the dull ache of sexual frustration seeping through his bones, he wanted more.

The image of two rosy-tipped breasts came to mind as the bells of Westminster rang out the hour of one across the slumbering city, and he smiled into the darkness as his horses slowed at the corner between Pall Mall and St James's Square.

Opening Lucy's letter on her return home, Emerald found the missive to be full of the adolescent adulation Asher Wellingham had spoken of. After memorising the note for future reference and consigning it to the fire, she walked across to the window to watch the sky.

Tonight the heavens were clear, a half-formed moon low in the eastern horizon and climbing. It would rain tomorrow, she suspected, for a cloud of mist encircled the glowing crescent and the air had a tang of moisture in it.

She wondered where the Duke of Carisbrook was now. Entwined in the arms of the green-eyed woman, she guessed, and wondered why she found the thought so irritating.

Asher Wellingham was nothing to her.

She would be in and out of Falder in a matter of days, hours even, if her searching went to plan. And then she would be gone. Away from here. Away from him.

Her mind wandered to the feel of his arms around her waist as they had danced tonight, the soft music between them. She had leant her head against the superfine of his jacket and breathed in.

'Lord,' she said aloud and swore roundly. Is this what England was making her? Soft? Needy? Dependent?

She was her father's daughter with years of fighting imbued in her blood and drawn upon her skin. Her finger went to the mark that intersected her right eyebrow and travelled beneath her fringe into her scalp. Black Jack Porrit and his men off the coast of Barranquilla in the winter of 1819. She would never fit in here and before the first whisper of her parentage surfaced in London town she would need to be gone.

With resolve she stripped off the gown and arranged her blankets beside the window overlooking the street.

Across the city the bells peeled in the night. Two o'clock. Burrowing down, she whispered the name of her sister into the darkness.

'Soon, Ruby. I will be home soon. I promise.'

Chapter Five

Miriam and Emerald arrived at Falder just as a rain shower departed and the sun tinged the clouds off the wild coast of Fleetness Point.

Falder.

To Emerald it was the most beautiful land she had ever seen, soft green hills with glades of trees colouring the lay of the fields. Everything about it was appealing. The isolation. The strength. The way the valleys dipped to a sea that was cold and free and deep. She could smell the sharp taste of salt on the wind and hear the lonely voices of the gulls.

Home. Home. Home.

Falder beckoned to her in a doleful wailing chant. Breathing in, she caught her reflection in the window of the coach and screwed up her nose. Would she ever get used to the shortness of her hair?

'If the master of Falder discovers any more about us we will be tossed out in a minute.' Miriam fidgeted with the thin silk strap of the little reticule she carried. 'And if you think to dress in your lad's clothes and scour the house at night, I should warn you of the dangers in it.'

Taking a deep breath, Emerald rubbed her palms against the rough wool of her cape. 'Would you rather I took a knife to his throat, Aunt?' Today, in the light of what she had to pretend, she could not find it in herself to be kind.

'You would kill him?'

'No, of course not,' she answered back and swallowed down chagrin. Lord, did Miriam truly think that she was capable of slitting the jugular of an unarmed man?

'Beau made some stupid mistakes, Emerald. And I would say his biggest one was not dispatching you to England the moment your mother left.'

'I think sometimes you are too hard on my father—' she began, but Miriam would have none of it.

'You were six and he was away as often as he was not.'

'I had Azziz and St Clair.'

'Pah! That huge house and a boy who barely spoke the English language. You think that was a suitable home?'

'It was my home.' How often before had they had this very same conversation?

'Your home? With a bevy of Beau's good-time girls and barely a night without some drunken orgy?'

'He missed my mother.'

'Missed her money more like.'

Emerald frowned. This was a tangent she had not heard before. 'Money. My mother had money?'

Miriam paled. 'I promised my brother that I would never talk of that time. He wanted you to be free of the restraints and vagaries of society and I promised him my silence.' Shifting in her seat, she crossed herself and Emerald saw the glimpse of a tear. 'He was a man who demanded too much sometimes. Even of me.'

'I do not even have a name to remember her by, Miriam. Can you not give me just that?'

'Evangeline.'

When the dark eyes of her aunt met her own she felt a heady dizzy sense of shock.

'Evangeline.' She whispered it, turning the word on her tongue. Savouring it. At last a name. 'Like an angel?'

Miriam's deep frown was not quite what she had expected. 'Your mother found life away from England difficult, and my brother would not have been the easiest of husbands. But he was your father and my brother and one should never speak ill of the dead, God bless them all.'

As the silence lengthened Emerald knew that she would hear no more.

Falder was a revelation. An uninhibited and magnificent hotchpotch of architectural styles, it sat above a river on a hillock completely surrounded by grassland. Part-Scottish baronial, part-Gothic and part-English manor, its many turrets and gables dominated the landscape around it and proclaimed not only great wealth, but a long lineage of generations of Caris-brooks who had all added their mark to it.

As the carriage clattered in across a pebbled drive, she looked up and hoped that there were not too many other guests here this weekend, for she was beginning to feel that she could not brave another round of social niceties.

A bevy of servants were at the front entrance to meet them, their faces stiff with the rigours of servitude; she refrained from meeting their glances, reasoning that such folk might be better at recognising a faux lady should they come across one. The thought made her frown. Circumstance had robbed her of being gently reared, but her birth was hardly dubious. Beau had been a lord before he had become a pirate and the title of Lady was hers to rightly use. She took the arm of her aunt and started up the staircase.

Asher Wellingham was waiting in a small blue salon directly off the portico. Beside him another tall man stood.

'Was your journey here pleasant?' The Duke asked the question in a voice that was measured.

'Thank you, yes, it was.' Emerald helped Miriam to a chair on one side of the fireplace and arranged a woollen blanket across her lap. Her aunt looked pale and tired and old, a woman whose secrets had leached the lifeblood from her soul. Her father's sister, her only relative left save for Ruby. In the unfamiliarity of Falder she was suddenly dear. Standing, she draped one arm protectively across Miriam's frail shoulders as Asher

Wellingham apologized for his mother's absence—she was indisposed—and introduced his brother.

Taris Wellingham wore thick glasses and stood with his hand against the end of a large armoire. The identical sense of danger that cloaked his brother cloaked him and he had exactly the same shade of hair: midnight black. She waited for him to give his greeting, but he did not.

'Taris had an accident off the coast of the Caribbean. You may need to come closer.' The Duke's sentence was offered so flatly that Emerald's mouth widened at the rudeness.

'I am sorry—' she stammered loudly and was cut off.

'My brother is not deaf.' A sense of challenge filled the room, unspoken and sharp. Miriam pushed back in her chair, but Emerald took two steps forward and waited as opaque eyes ran across her. She had a feeling he saw more than she wanted him to.

'Your voice holds the accent of a place very far from here, Lady Emma?'

She stayed silent, loath to lie to a man who had been so badly hurt, the scar across his forehead dissecting his left eye and running down the line of his cheek. The mark of a bullet! No small accident this one. Could he have been another casualty of her father's? The thought worried her unduly and she was relieved when a maid offered them a drink.

Miriam preferred lemonade, but Emerald chose white wine; taking a sip to calm her nerves, she made herself stand straighter, caring little for her added height.

'Asher tells us that your cousin Liam saved our sister from ruination.' The line of Taris's eyes did not quite meet her own.

'Well, I would hardly say ruination.'

'Would you not?' Asher Wellingham's question was underlaid with anger. 'Your cousin is a hero, albeit a reluctant one. What ship did you say he took to the Americas?'

'The *Cristobel*,' she returned without pause, glad that she had taken the time before coming up to Falder to check the shipping schedules, though as she gave the name another thought surfaced. What if he checked the passenger list and found no mention of Liam Kingston and his family? Or worse—what if he discovered that she had been into the shipping office making enquiry as to the departures?

Complicity and subterfuge.

She had a feeling that the Duke of Carisbrook would take badly to them both and she was being increasingly drawn into a web of deceit.

A sennight, she mused. Seven days to find the map and leave. If she were quick, everything would be feasible, but if she were not…?

'Your house is beautiful,' she said as her eyes scoured this room and the next one for any sign of what she was after. 'How many rooms does it have?'

'One hundred and twenty-seven,' Lucinda supplied the information. 'We have two libraries and a ballroom and Asher has just had a new fencing room added to the eastern wing that was built three years ago.'

Filing away the information, Emerald thought she should perhaps start looking over the new wing, although the salons radiating out from this room looked promising. She would start here tonight and then plan a general widening of her search as a grid, so that no room would be forgotten.

Two hours later she was ensconced in a bedchamber overlooking the front drive of the house. Miriam was in the room next to her and had used a headache as an excuse to take herself to bed. Emerald hoped that she was not sickening with a cold, or worse; wandering over to wide doors curtained with billowing yards of soft fabric, she opened the latch. Sunlight streamed in unbroken across a balcony draped in ivy. Walking outside, she was perfectly still. The sound of long beaching waves rolling in from the northern seas could be heard and, if she stood on her tiptoes, there in the distance, between the crease of two green hillocks, she saw the ocean, dancing and sparkling in the sun. The ocean. Her ocean, the warm blue of the Caribbean mixed with the wilder grey of Fleetness Point.

A noise had her looking down as Asher Wellingham rounded the corner on a large horse. Moving back into the room, she watched him until he was out of sight, the fluid muscle of his racing stallion reflected in the surface of the lake as he passed it, a dark shadow against a darker line of the trees.

He was a man who did not seem to fit into the strict regimens of London's manners or its rules, a duke who seemed more dangerous than he had any right to be, and more menacing. She smiled. Now there was a word that described Asher Wellingham exactly.

Menacing.

And she would need to be very, very careful.

He was dressed in black at dinner and his hair was wet. The length of it was intriguing. Too short to be easily tied into a queue, but far longer than most other men of the *ton* wore theirs.

As they filed in to the dining room, Emerald found herself seated to Asher's left, his sister acting as hostess, in his mother's continued absence, at the foot of the table with Taris to her left. An older couple made up the numbers, near neighbours invited for the evening, for Miriam had decided not to come down and had asked to have a tray delivered to her.

'Is your room satisfactory, Lady Emma?' Lucy asked as the steaming plates of food were brought to the table. Beef, pork and chicken. When her stomach rumbled she pushed down on it hard and hoped that nobody had heard.

'It's very beautiful and I can see the ocean from the balcony,' she added, frowning as Asher looked up sharply. Tonight he looked tired. She saw that he was drinking heavily, saw too the gesture Lucy made to the servant behind to bring her brother a carafe of water. He didn't touch it.

'Emma hails from Jamaica,' he said as the silence grew.

The man named William Bennett nodded. 'I was there once, a long time ago. Did you know a family by the name of de la Varis?'

'No, I don't believe so. My father was an invalid, so we were quite insular.' For a second she wondered how it would be best to keep track of all the lies and decided that later she would write out her fabrications in a diary. Relaxing into the role, she picked up her confidence and continued. 'My aunt and uncle lived close by and I had Liam, of course. My cousin,' she qualified as the man looked puzzled.

'And your own mother?'

'Oh, she was a beautiful woman. Evangeline.' Emerald enunciated the newness of the name lovingly and just the saying of it conjured up a golden-haired beauty to stand alongside her sick but handsome father. She smiled. She had always filled her world with dream people. When her mother had gone. When her father had returned with yet another woman whom she insisted she call mama.

Dreams had saved them all and made them whole and good and true. It was not so hard here to imagine cousins or a beautiful mother who had not deserted her.

'Liam is about your age, then?' Lucy's query was strongly voiced. Of all the Carisbrooks she was the most inquisitive.

'No, he is a little older,' she replied evasively, trying to remember the exact number of offspring she had invented for her fictitious cousin. Would 'a little older' render such children possible? Had she said four?

'And did he like to read, Lady Emma?' Lucy continued.

'Like to read?' Danger spiralled.

'I think my sister is referring to the books in your aunt's drawing room.' When Lucy smiled and nodded, interest sharpened in his eyes. 'Miriam does not strike me as a scholar of Arabic philosophy.'

'And you think that I would be?' She forced a laugh and was rewarded with a *frisson* of uncertainty. 'Indeed, your Grace, the books were my father's.'

'Ahh, yes of course. The devout and invalided scholar?'

Emerald wondered at the edge of disbelief she could plainly hear and was relieved when Lucinda again garnered her attention.

'I should like to sketch you while you are here, if I may, Lady Emma.'

Emerald looked up sharply. Was she jesting? Dangerous ground this. She didn't know quite how to answer. How easy would it be for Lucy to fathom the memory of Liam Kingston in her face? 'Are there many of your works here at Falder?'

'That one is mine.' Her hand pointed to a large watercolour above the fireplace depicting the castle and Emerald caught her breath.

'You have a considerable talent. Do you sell them?'

'No, but I gave Jack Henshaw one once as a gift and Saul Beauchamp. Asher's friends,' she clarified as Emerald looked puzzled. 'I have not mustered up the courage to show them further, but if you would like a look at some other portraits I have done I would be more than pleased to show you.'

Portraits? Of her brother, perhaps? Emerald felt a rising interest until she saw the dark anger that coated Asher Wellingham's eyes.

She was pleased when the servants began to clear away the plates and the women were able to repair to the smaller salon.

Taris sat against the window and placed his hand on the cold hard surface of the glass. From where he stood, Asher could see the outline of mist that surrounded his print. He wondered just how much of it Taris could also see. Today he had tripped over a stool in the study. A year ago he would have walked straight around it.

'Emma Seaton is not as she seems.'

Asher stiffened and waited for clarification.

'No, she is stronger than she pretends to be. Much stronger.' He paused for a moment before continuing. 'Describe her for me, Asher. What does she look like?'

'Her eyes are the colour of the sea, she has the shortest hair I have ever seen on a woman and she never removes her gloves.'

'Why not?'

'God knows why, for I certainly don't.'

Taris began to smile. 'And her face?'

'You could see nothing of her?'

'I could hear that she is beautiful.'

'That she is.'

Taris's sudden laughter unnerved him. 'And when was the last time you thought a woman beautiful?'

As Asher walked away from a discussion he did not want, he fingered the sapphire ring he wore on his little finger and cursed his brother.

Chapter Six

Emerald dressed in black trousers and a jacket, stuffing a candle and tinder box into its deep pockets. It was already after three and the last sounds of people moving had been well over an hour ago.

She had memorised the layout of the rooms that she had been in, but was glad for a full moon. The light slanted against her as the curtain opened and she stepped out on to the balcony.

Night time.

She had always loved the darkness, even as a child, and here the sounds of the countryside after the stuffiness of London were welcomed. Shimmying down the ivy that hung from the latticed balcony, she crept around the edges of the lawn, careful to walk where the vegetation overlaid the grass so her footprints would not show. At the wide door that accessed the library from the garden she paused and drew out a piece of wire. Slotting it into the lock, she was glad to hear the mechanism turn and the portal spring open.

One minute at most.

Letting herself into the room, she stood against the velvet curtain and waited until her eyes had become accustomed to the darkness before lighting the candle.

Bookcase upon bookcase greeted her, the leather-bound copies of a thousand volumes lending the musky scent of learning to the air. Her fingers ran across the embossed titles closest to her: Milton, Shakespeare, Webster, Donne and Johnson. A library that embraced great authors and their ideas. She wondered which of the Carisbrooks was the reader and guessed it to be Asher, the thought making her smile.

A low shelf to one side of the room caught her attention. Rolls of paper were stacked against a cupboard and behind them there was an alcove containing other things. Umbrellas, parasols and walking sticks.

Her heart began to hammer. Could it be this easy? She held her breath as she sorted through the objects. A stick of ebony, another of some fragrant wood and a third handmade, using the shiny limbs of birch. Her father's cane with the map inside it was not among them. Neither was it in the next room nor the next one.

Some time later she knew that she would be pressing her luck to keep searching. Already she had heard the stirrings of the servants in the kitchens and knew very soon other maids would come to set the fires or draw the curtains. Creeping out of the room she was in, she found herself in a smaller salon with a row of windows gracing one wall—it was then that she saw it.

The first light of pale dawn slanted across a portrait. A portrait of the Duke of Carisbrook and a woman. Her Grace, Melanie, the Duchess of Carisbrook, the title written beneath it said, and she was beautiful.

Melanie. As in the ship that was ready to launch in London? Asher's wife? A red-haired beauty with eyes the colour of midnight. Emerald could not keep from studying the face.

What had happened to her? Where was she? The date on the painting was from ten years ago and she would have been merely the age that Emerald was now. Who could she ask? Lucinda, perhaps. Quietly, of course. She ran her fingers across the thick swirl of paint that made up a brocade skirt and looked again at the painting. Asher Wellingham's hair was short and he was young. As young as his wife and in love. She could see it in the light of his eyes and in the way his hand curled around hers, holding them together in an eternal embrace.

And the ring that Melanie Wellingham sported on her marriage finger was the same ring that Asher Wellingham now wore on his little finger.

An unexpected noise to one end of the room had her turning and she left the house with only the slightest of whispers.

Asher stood against the door to the small salon and watched Emma Seaton blow out her candle and slide through the opened window with all the expertise and finesse of a consummate thief. Hardly a noise, barely a footprint. He had thought her an intruder at first until the light from the flame had thrown her high cheek-bones into relief.

What the hell was she doing here? He walked across to stand where she had just been, in front of the picture above the mantel, and his heart wrenched with sadness.

The wedding portrait painted just after they had returned from their honeymoon in Scotland. God. It had been so many years ago now he could barely recognise the man he was then. Cursing, he turned away and went to the window, watching as a shadow, black against the pearly dawn, flitted around the edge of the house leaving no trace of its presence. No sign of what he could not believe that he had seen.

Who was she?

A thief? A robber? Something more sinister?

Another wilder thought surfaced. What had Lucinda said of Liam Kingston? Tall. Accented. Thin.

Emma Seaton.

Hell! There was no Liam Kingston. It had always been her. The Countess of Haversham had certainly appeared bemused by Emma's insistence on a cousin. And now he knew why.

He almost laughed at the ruse and would have marched to her room then and there and confronted her had not another thought stopped him.

She had saved his sister.

She had risked her own life for the well-being of a

stranger. The bruise on her cheek. Her embarrassment. Her ridiculous story as to how it had happened.

She had saved Lucinda from certain damnation and ruination and she had demanded nothing in return.

Why?

He would find out.

But first he had to determine whether Lady Emma Seaton posed a danger to his family. Starting from today.

The Duke of Carisbrook was still at the table when Emerald went down to breakfast later that morning. Folding his paper, he waited as she gave the hovering servant her preference of beverage.

'I trust you slept well last night.'

She smiled at his query and helped herself to a slice of toast from the rack in the centre of the table. 'Oh, indeed I did, your Grace. It must be the country air.' She yawned widely.

'And your bed was comfortable?'

'Very.'

'You were not disturbed by any noises in the night?'

She gave him a sideways look to determine where this line of questioning might be leading. 'No, I certainly was not. Why, as soon as my head hits the pillow I am generally asleep and stay so until the morning.'

'You are most fortunate, then.'

'You do not sleep well?'

'I don't.' He raised his cup of coffee to his lips and peered at her over the rim. When his eyes locked on to hers, it was she who looked away, making much of buttering her toast. He might suspect her, but that was all. And tonight, forewarned of his lightness of sleep, she would be far more careful in her searching.

'I was planning a ride across the fields of Falder. Would you like to accompany me? Lucy has a spare riding skirt and jacket and you will find anything else you need in the room off the stables.'

'I'm not certain. It has been a long time since I was on a horse.'

'We will go slowly, Lady Emma.'

Emerald frowned, for beneath the outward affinity there was a look that held a hint of something much darker. A rage kept only in check by a steel-strong will. She tried to keep the conversation light.

'Lucinda said your mother resides here in Falder but I have yet to meet her. She also said that the Dowager Duchess enjoys keeping bad health.'

He smiled at that, the white of his teeth startling against the tan on his face.

'That she does. Lucinda surprises me sometimes with her insights into others. Take your cousin for instance.' A gleam of something she could not quite interpret danced in his eyes. 'Liam Kingston. She saw him as an honourable man. A man who would not lie. A trait of character to be commended in a person, would you not say?'

'Indeed, I would.' She hoped he did not hear the waver in her voice.

'Indeed, you would,' he repeated and lifted a silver knife to take jam from the pot before him. He used his left hand for almost everything, she noted. Writing. Smoking. Eating. The hand that was not ruined.

Her mind went back to the day they had boarded his ship and she took in a short breath. He had once been right-handed. She was certain of it. The enormity of the realisation made her stiffen. When had the accident happened? Lord, not straight after she had toppled him overboard? Surely not right then.

'My family is extremely important to me, Lady Emma, and as the head of the house it is my duty to see that they remain safe.'

'I see.' The beat of her heart was twice its normal speed and rising.

'I'm glad that you do.' The smile that he gave her did not reach his eyes.

'Good morning.'

Lucinda's voice had Emerald turning in relief. Asher's questions had an edge to them that she didn't understand—it was as if he was furious at her. An awful thought surfaced. Could he have seen her last night? She had heard a noise as she had left the small room off the library, though she was certain that if he had seen her she would hardly be sitting here and being served a very substantial breakfast. With growing unease she looked across at Lucy.

Today Asher's sister was dressed in a deep-blue riding habit and had a wide smile on her face. A complete and utter contrast to her own, she supposed, and was unreasonably tired by such innocence and openness.

Petty, she knew, and belittling to honour. Taking a breath, she tried to rally.

'Are you joining us for breakfast, Lucy?' Asher asked as he pushed out a chair for his sister.

'No, I have already eaten. Taris said you would be going into the village this morning and I thought to ride with you, for I am spending the day with Rodney and Annabelle Graveson. Will you be leaving soon?'

'As soon as we have breakfasted.'

The cold lash of his eyes gave Emerald the feeling that he was ordering her to go with him for this had nothing to do with choice. Swallowing her gall, she squared her shoulders and faced Lucy. If the Duke of Carisbrook meant to confront her, she would rather the scene take place away from Falder. 'Your brother mentioned a riding habit of yours that I might use?'

'Of course. Come with me now and we can find it—I have just the colour to go with your hair. Dark green—have you ever worn that colour? You tend more to the pastels, you see, and I thought really the deeper shades might just suit you better. The tone of your hair is unusual. Not quite blonde, but not red either. Do you take after your mother?'

Shaking her head at all the questions, Emerald followed Lucy from the room, glad to have a genuine reason to leave.

An hour later they were wending their way into Thornfield. After a shaky start Emerald had picked up her old skills in riding and was enjoying the freedom of being on horseback. Lucinda beside her chatted about her childhood; in front of them Taris rode a little further back from his brother. She could see how he concentrated on the path before him and on the sounds of the horse's hooves upon the road. Lucy sometimes called out to him, warning him of an incline or of a particularly deep ditch.

Asher gave him nothing. No help. No leeway. She wondered what it was Taris had been doing off the coast of the Caribbean when he had lost his sight.

Thornfield was beautiful. A village set beside the sea with a main road sporting a number of shops and many well-built houses, round a deep harbour where a ship was moored.

As Asher dismounted and helped his sister down, Emerald was already fastening the reins of her horse and looking towards the ship.

'It is yours?'

'Ours,' he amended. 'She's the *Nautilus*, built for the Eastern Line and due out to India at the end of the month to fill a silk contract we have in Calcutta.'

'She's beautiful. What does she draw?'

'You know something about ships?'

Cursing her slip, she lied easily. 'Liam was always interested in ships, so I suppose some of his knowledge must have rubbed off on to me.' Deliberately she turned away from the harbour and perused the inn, glad that the brim on the hat she wore was wide, for she doubted she could have hidden the longing she was consumed with.

To set foot on a ship again. To ride in the winds of a wide-open sea with the smell of salt and adventure close to the bone. To climb up the rigging of an eighty-foot mast and hang suspended against the blueness of a horizon that stretched for ever.

A voice calling to them brought her from her thoughts and she looked around to see a man hurrying forward.

'I had hoped to see you here today, your Grace,' he said when he was upon them. 'There was a break-in on the *Nautilus* last night, though from what I can gather nothing was taken. But the lock on the main cabin door was forced and a few papers shifted.'

'Did anyone see anything untoward?'

'No, nothing. Davis heard noises after midnight and thought it was me checking on the ropes.'

'Set a double shift tonight, then,' Asher ordered, 'and have Silas bring his dog back on board.'

Emerald stiffened as his eyes raked across her and again she felt some sense of complicity and an uncertainty that was hard to pin down. Had Azziz and Toro frisked the ship already? It could well be possible. She had determined to contact them tonight and let them know of the new plans Asher Wellingham had set in place to guard his ship when the arrival of a beautifully dressed woman in her forties made her turn. At her side there walked a boy, his eyes firmly fixed on Lucinda.

'I didn't realise that you would be up for the week, Asher.' The woman smiled, looking at Emerald and waiting for an introduction.

'Lady Emma Seaton, meet Lady Annabelle Graveson

and her son, Rodney. Emma is newly come to London to stay with her aunt, the Countess of Haversham.'

'Miriam of Haversham?' Her glance sharpened on the locket around Emerald's neck; if she had been pale before, now she was even more so.

'You are her niece?' Her fingers pulled at the lace around her collar before her eyes rolled up and she fell into the arms of Asher Wellingham.

Again, Emerald thought.

How tiring it must be to for ever have collapsing women swoon around you. This faint, however, hardly looked like the one she had pretended in the Henshaw ballroom. It was obvious that Annabelle Graveson was truly ill for her face had taken on a greenish-grey pallor and sweat covered her brow.

Asher Wellingham hardly seemed fazed as he lifted the woman up effortlessly and led the small contingent into the inn, where a space was cleared on a cushioned seat.

'Fetch some water and give us some room,' he ordered and the innkeeper wasted no time in doing as he was bid.

Rodney stood at the foot of his mother's makeshift bed. 'She said that she felt ill this morning, but I didn't think she meant this ill.' Emerald noticed Lucy's hand resting on his shoulder, trying to give him comfort and almost laughed.

This ill?

The woman was probably just hot or the stays binding her stick-thin waist were too tight. Already she was coming to. She thought back to the aftermath of battles aboard the *Mariposa* when sailors had sat in silence against the bulwarks and nursed broken bones. Or worse.

But this was England, she reminded herself, where a faint still retained an important place in the whole scheme of things. A vivid reminder of the place of fragile women.

She watched as the woman sat herself up and wiped her brow and upper lip with a delicate hanky she had extracted from the sleeve at her wrist.

'Oh, my goodness,' she said, repeating it over again as she looked around the group. 'I said to Rodney this morning that I was not feeling up to a jaunt into the village. My stomach, you understand. It is rather unpredictable and yesterday the cook served a strong soup that I can only surmise was badly made. Old meat, if I were to hazard a guess, or fungi plucked from a place it should not have been. Rodney, where are you?'

'I am here, Mama.' He did not move and Emerald looked away when she perceived that both Annabelle Graveson and her son were watching her, their blue eyes a mirror copy of each other's.

Asher, as usual, had taken charge, ordering large platters of food and wine and making certain that Taris was aware of the fare that was placed before him. Glancing across the room, she saw a group of young men looking her way, but the scorching glance of the Duke of Carisbrook discouraged them.

She almost smiled. How easy it must be to slip into the role of a protected woman.

How simply easy.

Lucinda. Annabelle Graveson. They let him take charge without even noticing what they had given up.

'Are you at Falder for long, Lady Emma?' Rodney Graveson was sitting on her left side, next to Lucinda.

'For a week. My aunt, the Countess of Haversham, is here, too, but she has been laid low by a cough and has taken to her bed. Perhaps you know of her—your mother seems to.'

'Mama seldom travels outside of Thornfield these days, but I have heard her mention that name.'

He blushed, his fair hair standing out against the colour, but he did not look away and Emerald liked him for it. Once, years ago, she too had been cursed with such shyness and Rodney Graveson seemed like a kindred spirit and in desperate need of friendship. Looking up, she caught Annabelle Graveson watching her.

'What is it you are speaking of with Lady Emma, Rodney?' Her voice was high and the colour in her cheeks was better.

'He was just asking me how long I planned to be here for, Lady Annabelle.'

'Oh, I see. And your answer?'

'Seven days, I think.'

'Then we shall have you over to Longacres for dinner next Sunday. Asher will bring you. About six.'

She did not ask the others at the table, which struck Emerald as both odd and rather impolite, and the Duke of Carisbrook's perfunctory nod was such that she wondered if he meant to honour the invitation at all, but as she felt the squeeze of Rodney Graveson's hand against her own beneath the table she was touched by his gesture and hoped that it would be possible to go.

Two hours later, after saying goodbye to the others Emerald sat on Hercules and picked her way down the incline behind Asher Wellingham on his tall black stallion. Lucy had stayed in Thornfield with the Gravesons and Taris had met a friend at the tavern and had decided to embark on a game of chess. Emerald wondered whether the whole thing had been a set-up, for Asher Wellingham seemed very keen on riding back with her and left as soon as the first opportunity presented itself. She also wondered as to the propriety of being alone with him, but dismissed that notion with indifference. Her reputation here was unimportant—she would be gone from England as soon as she found the cane.

The sea lay before them and, licking her lips, she could taste the salt. Here the sand was not fine and white, but grey and coarse, the pebbles mulched by the movement of this lonely, lovely coast. The sea. Her heart sang at the joy of being beside it again. If this was my home, she thought, I should never leave it.

After the warning at breakfast Asher Wellingham had seemed withdrawn and quiet. He did not tarry or offer her any explanation of beaches, cliffs or field.

His land, she thought.

If he loved Falder, it was not obvious.

'What is the peninsula in the distance?' she asked as the sun lit up a long low tongue of land to their left.

'The Eddington Finger,' he said promptly. 'Though my great-great-grandfather always called it "Return Home Bay." The last sight of Falder lands as he left the coast, I suppose. He was a sailor with a love for adventure.'

He stopped as they cantered down on to the sand and dismounted and the image of an old duke naming the place made Emerald laugh.

'What was his name? Your great-great-grandfather's name,' she qualified when he looked puzzled.

'Ashland. My father was Ashborne and his father Ashton, all derivatives of the original family name of Ashalan. It is tradition.'

'Tradition.' Longing welled on her face. She was certain he must have seen it and was surprised when he smiled. It made him look younger, as young as he had looked on his ship off Turks Island with the sea winds at his back. As young as the man staring out from the portrait in the small salon with a loving wife on his arm.

Desire snaked through caution and she was shocked by the heavy hammering of her heart. She, who had been around men all her life. Handsome men. Dangerous men. But none like this one. None who had haunted her dreams for five long years with his velvet eyes and night-black hair. None who spoke of a family name that they could trace back through the generations and whose ancestral seat rivalled that of any lord of the realm.

Responsibility and place.

A combination that became all the more appealing with the land of his birth at his back and the full blue day upon his face. Her own shifting lifestyle completed the equation. What must it be like to have your children run in the same fields as their children and their children's children? Oh, tradition was sweet when you had never had it.

The silence between them stretched in an endless vacuum as he helped her dismount and she felt a breathless shiver of wonder. Did he feel it too? How could he not? She was shocked at her thoughts, shocked at the sheer bald desire for his touch. Schooling herself to wait as he tethered the horses to a branch, she was surprised at his first question.

'What were you doing in the blue salon last night, Lady Emma?'

'Last night?' She hoped the slight catch in her voice would be interpreted as chagrin rather than the bone-deep fear she was suddenly consumed with.

'Last night when you slipped through the rooms of my house in the guise of one suspiciously similar to the description my sister gave of Liam Kingston.' He was very still.

'I am not certain what you mean.' With her back against the wall she couldn't afford to give an inch.

He changed tack, easily. Distrust coated his words and was seen in the hard planes of his face. 'What is it you want from me?'

'Want from you? Nothing, your Grace. And there is a simple explanation for last night. I have never slept well since my father's passing. Sometimes in the dead of night I wander…'

'Dressed as a boy and moving in and out of the house like a shadow. I think not.'

One hand encircled her wrist and she felt the same bolt of awareness that she was almost becoming used to in his company.

'Are you a thief?' he asked quietly, his thumb caressing the sensitive skin at her wrist.

'No.' The touch of his breath across the sensitive folds of her neck nearly undid her.

'A spy, then? Who sent you here?' His fingers tightened. Not a harsh hold, but a tempered one. She knew he must feel the hammering pulse beneath his fingers.

'No one.' She could barely get the words out.

'I do not believe you, but if you are in trouble I could help.'

It was the last thing she had expected him to say.

He hardly knew her and yet here he was offering his assistance. Another responsibility. Another needy supplicant. Another duty on top of all his other duties. Pride made her shake her head and she saw a distinct flicker of relief.

'You are a guest here at Falder and my sister would be disappointed, no doubt, if I packed you off before your due date of departure. But if you sleepwalk again, Lady Emma, take warning, for I shall not be as lenient as I have been this time. Do I make myself clear?'

'Perfectly.'

'Then I'm glad of it.' Again, his thumb traced the

blue veins on the thin skin of her wrist and she felt her world throb. When she looked up, there was muted calculation in his eyes and a worm of worry niggled.

Had he used the caress as a means to an end by underlining his threat with a promise? Admiration surfaced in equal proportions with ire. Such cunning would not be out of place on board the *Mariposa*, for with it he had gained exactly what he wanted.

And all without raising a finger. She was too much her father's daughter not to applaud his craftiness.

Taking her reins when he offered them back, she walked her horse down towards the water, the mist of salt enveloping the beach with an opaque whiteness. A wilder bay than she was used to, and colder. Shivering, she bent to pick up a shell and the sound inside as she raised it to her ear was exactly the same as it was at home.

For a second she felt displaced, uncertain, lost in the pull of what had been taken from her, and drawn to the man who now came to stand beside her, his cheeks lightly spattered with the mist of ocean. If she had been braver, she might have leant forward and touched the wetness, felt the swell of cheek beneath her fingers, and understood what it was that she could now only guess at. But she was not brave. Not like that. Not here with the wide brim of her hat tugging in the wind and the fullness of her riding skirt unfamiliar around her legs.

Don't. Don't. Don't.

She recited the word over again and again beneath her breath, trying to incite some sort of sense in her actions. Trying to make herself step back from him, out of reach, out of harm, out of temptation. But when his thumb came up to caress the sensitive skin on her bottom lip, she closed her eyes and just felt.

For once.

For this once.

For the time it took to run her tongue across the length of skin and bring his flesh into her mouth.

'Lord, what you do to me.' The darkness in his eyes was bottomless as his lips slanted down across her own, the hunger in them easily definable in the afternoon grey. Just the two of them with the damp rivulets of water running beneath her feet, and the green lands of England all around. Just the two of them coming together along the full lines of their bodies and pressing hard.

And then there was nothing.

No today or yesterday, or tomorrow with its sharp uncertainty.

Just him. Just the warmth of skin against the cool of the rain and the burning fiery want that consumed her. She did not notice when he cast aside her hat, loosening the curls to his touch. All she knew was urgency and want and need.

A man's touch. On her woman's body. The living reality of her countless dreams. She felt the puckering of her nipples and the clench of an almost-pain between her legs.

More. More.

Everything, she longed to whisper, everything, and when he drew away she tried to hold on, tried to take his mouth in the same way that he had taken hers, but he stopped her simply by pulling her against him, head firm beneath his chin, fitting well into the spaces of his body.

'Emma.' Whispered. Barely there.

The frantic beat of his heart against his throat told her that he was as affected as she was. Not all one-sided, then, not all her fault. She could not find it in herself to raise her eyes to his.

'I'm sorry. That should not have happened.' His voice was husky. 'There is no excuse at all. I should not have—' He stopped and the shrill cry of a gull could be heard over the silence.

He was sorry? She stiffened. An apology. For this? Every man she had ever known in her life would have taken what it was she had just offered and be damned with what happened next. But not Asher Wellingham. No, not him. Confusion ripped through guilt and sheer embarrassment chased hard on the heels of that.

Lord. What now? When she felt his hands slacken she stepped back and reached for the bridle, angry at the help she needed to mount and pleased when he did not speak again as he handed her her hat. Did not explain. Did not even try to draw level with her as they cantered along the beach and up into the valley that led to Falder Castle.

Gaining her room she laid her head back against the solidness of the portal and tried to catch her breath, lost in the run up from the stables. Her breathing was closer to normal when she opened the connecting door to see Miriam sitting in a chair by her window, reading a book.

'Whatever has happened? You look like you have come across a ghost.'

Emerald's smile was laboured. Hardly a ghost. Asher's lips still burnt into the recesses of her memory and raised the temperature of everything.

Hot. Scorching. Torrid.

She poured herself some water, watching the drips run jagged against the side of the glass before drinking it all.

'You seem better, Aunt.'

'If you could find the cane, Emerald, I'd be better still.' The sentence was finished on a bout of coughing and Emerald's worry grew. After her behaviour today, she was uncertain whether the Duke of Carisbrook would even want her to stay till the end of the week and here was her aunt plagued with illness.

Lord, could things get any worse? She shook her head and made herself concentrate on what Miriam was saying.

'Carisbrook has a map room at the back of the eastern wing. I saw it today when I attempted a walk round the rose garden. Perhaps he has already found the map, and keeps it there.'

Emerald's interest was piqued. 'Near the rose garden you say?'

'Yes. The Wellingham family mausoleum sits further over to one side. The footman I walked with said that the garden has been laid out in memory of the Duchess of Carisbrook.'

'Melanie Wellingham is dead and buried at Falder?'

'She is indeed. The tomb of their son is there too.'

'A son?'

'Stillborn at full term three years before she died.'

Death and loss and waste.

The enormity of Miriam's revelations changed everything. The Duke of Carisbrook had loved his wife. He still loved his wife. The sapphire ring on his finger, the picture in the library and the flower garden, and his self-confessed resistance to being plunged again into the state of holy matrimony—suddenly everything added up, made sense.

She was a small detour in the course of his life. That was all. He was a duke with lands stretching hundreds of miles in every direction and a shipping fleet that plied the world.

He was not for her.

Would never be for her.

She reached into her pocket for the shell she had collected and wished that she could find the map and just go home.

Chapter Seven

He was drunk.

He knew he was by the way the portrait of Melanie that he sat in front of swam in and out of focus. He hated this painting. Hated the sheer memory of it. A brutal reminder of all that he had lost.

He should not have kissed Emma Seaton. Not like that. Not with the raging want in his blood and the sure damned knowledge of duplicity in his head. She was not as she said she was. She was a liar and a would-be thief. She was dangerous to his family. To him. To the world he had spun around himself ever since he had returned home, a slim wedge against chaos. He should kick her out, right now, before the calmer shifts of reason took hold and her turquoise eyes reeled him in like the sirens of Circe, haunting, familiar and undeniably false.

And yet he couldn't. He couldn't. He sighed and leant his head back against the wall wondering just why it was that he couldn't. Not just the warm willingness of her body or the sharp raw hit of lust that had floored him when her lips had met his. No, there was something else too. Something he had felt unexpectedly as he had held her on the beach against him. Something close and safe and right. Something that took away the cold for ever etched into his very bones and left a question of possibility.

'I thought that I might find you here. And drinking.' The heavy censure in Taris's words jarred his thoughts and Asher closed his eyes against it. Tonight his more usual reserve was lost under the fiery belly of too much whisky.

'When I was with Emma Seaton today…I forgot Melanie. For just one moment…I forgot her.'

He felt the stillness of his brother rather than saw it, but he was strangely relieved by the confession. Saying the words lessened the strength of them. Tonight he needed absolution.

'She is a beautiful woman, Asher, and Melanie has been dead for over three years. Why should you not admire her?'

'Because she's a liar. Because she was here the other night. Right here. Dressed as a boy. And because I think she and Liam Kingston are one and the same.'

'Lucinda's knight in shining armour? The one who bested Stephen Eaton? Lady Emma?'

'She has a tattoo on the soft skin of her right breast.'

'A tattoo?' Intrigue was plain in his brother's question.

'Of a butterfly. Done in blue.'

Taris began to laugh.

'I want her to stay here. At Falder. I want to protect her…'

The laughter abruptly stopped.

'Someone has hurt her,' Asher continued and stood, tripping over a low stool in front of him as he did so and veering towards the wall. Leaning against it, he was pleased to regain his balance. 'And she's frightened. I can see it in her eyes…sometimes…often…and I can hear it in her voice.'

A clock chimed in the next room and Asher counted the hours. Three o'clock. Two more hours till the dawn and the promise of sleep. Tonight it was all he could do to keep from closing his eyes and let slumber overtake him.

But he mustn't.

He knew he mustn't. Not until the dawn when the voices were softer and memory did not cut his equilibrium to the quick.

He slid down the wall, his knees drawn up before him. In defeat. The stubs of his severed fingers rested against his knee and he brought them up into his vision as if seeing them for the first time.

'Sometimes I can feel these fingers…ghost fingers touching things, feeling things. I used to think they'd gone to the place where Melanie was, a little part of me waiting with her till the rest could follow…and now…I don't want to follow them.' As he leant his head back, his eyes went to the uncurtained window, where he could see only an unbroken darkness and he hated the lack of control he could hear in his voice.

'Melanie would have wanted you to be happy again. Laugh again. Feel again.'

'Would she?' He stroked his finger down the thin crystal stem of his glass and almost laughed. 'I remember once in Scotland when she nearly fell into a raging river and I caught her and pulled her back. She said that if anything ever happened to me, she would be sad for ever. For ever. Such a long time…for ever.'

Taris was quiet. Asher noticed he had removed his glasses and put them into his pocket. Seeing with memory. All that his brother was left with now. Sometimes he hated Beau Sandford with such a passion that it worried him. The smarting scars across his back. Taris's loss of sight. Even in death the pirate haunted him.

'Go to sleep, Taris. I will be all right.'

'I could stay…'

'No.'

He was pleased when his brother left him to his familiar demons.

Emerald strolled back towards Falder after an early morning walk, and caught sight of a light burning low in the little salon off the library as she mounted the front steps. If Asher Wellingham was already up, she would speak with him about yesterday. She should not have kissed him, should not have been alone with him, could not believe what she had done. She, who had always been so circumspect in dealing with the opposite sex. Well, it needed to stop before she did something she knew she would regret and she meant to tell him so right now.

The Duke of Carisbrook was slumped on the floor when she pushed open the door, his back against the wall and an empty bottle beside him. Taris sat asleep in an armchair. Like a sentinel.

Turning back to Asher, she saw that he watched her, the intensity of his gaze startling. He made no move to stand up; with his cravat askew and with the stubble of a twelve-hour beard upon his face, he looked like some dark and dissolute angel.

'I am sorry,' she managed. 'I saw the light from outside and thought I might speak with you. About yesterday.'

'Perhaps another time would be better,' he returned softly, and she was relieved to hear a hint of something akin to humour in his voice.

'You are well?' She could barely just leave it here.

His eyes flicked to the window where the beams of a new day flooded in.

'Very well. Now,' he replied and pushed himself up. Emerald resisted an impulse to help him as he bent over, his hands clamped tightly about his head and holding everything together. She had seen enough hangovers to recognise that this was a bad one.

'Did you sleep at all last night?'

He shook his head, squinting against the light that caught him squarely from this angle.

A new thought struck her. *He never slept.* Her mind

ran over the times she had found him up, fully dressed, in the small hours just before the dawn.

After the ball. The first night she had searched Falder. This morning. Each time with a glass in his hand and the look of the damned in his eyes.

'My father had a remedy for too much drink.' Her resolve to confront him faltered under his vulnerability this morning and his eyebrows arched.

'A man of many varied talents, then,' he chided and crossed the room to replace a blanket across his brother that had fallen on to the floor. Taris barely moved as he did so, well wrapped in the arms of Morpheus.

What had they spoken of, Emerald wondered, in the dead of night? What kept them from warmer beds and a more comfortable slumber? Memories? Secrets? Her?

'Could you concoct this remedy for me?'

She was more than surprised by his request. 'I'd need herbs and sugar and milk.'

'We could find those in the kitchen. It's this way.'

He edged his way around her, careful not to touch, and opened the door. She saw he used the solidness of it to retain his balance.

The kitchen was enormous and extremely well appointed. Ten or so people of all genders, sizes and ages scraped, cleaned, cooked and chopped, the smell of a fine luncheon permeating the air. A woman extracted herself from the others, wiping her hands on her apron as she came forward.

'Your Grace?' There was question in her voice. 'I hope all is well with the food...'

'Indeed it is, Mrs Tonner. But Lady Emma would like a few ingredients to make a drink.' He did not say what sort of drink.

'A drink?' Amazement overcame the cook's reserve. 'You wish to cook, my lady?'

'I wish to make a potion with eggs, milk and hyssop. And mandrake root, if you have it.'

A smile lit up Mrs Tonner's face. The secret recipe of Beau's was not just confined to the wilds of Jamaica, Emerald determined, and followed her to a well-stocked pantry where she quickly found what was needed. A smaller maid produced a bowl and whisk and another a large tumbler embossed with Asher Carisbrook's initials.

A.W. Not just his initials, either, but the sum of generations before him. Ashton Wellingham. Ashland Wellingham. Ashborne Wellingham.

Thanking the cook, she set to work, flustered when she saw that he meant to stay and watch her. The kitchen was as quiet as the dead, though ten sets of ears were fastened on their every movement and word.

'Did you make this often?' he asked as she worked. *Often and often and often.*

'No. Only a very few times when a parishioner was in his cups at church. Apart from that…' She let the sentence peter out as a vision of Beau downing the concoction in ever-increasing quantities overcame her.

Her father had been a mean drunk and a series of harlots had taken the brunt of his temper.

Mostly.

She was pleased that Asher was not of that ilk. Indeed, drink seemed to mellow him, make him easier to talk with, more vulnerable.

'Yet you can remember the recipe by heart?'

'It is a simple one, which you have to drink all at once.' She handed the tumbler to him as she finished.

He sniffed it and looked up. 'Is it supposed to smell this way?'

'Yes.' She tried to stop laughter as she registered his incredulity but could not quite. 'Strong liquor requires a strong antidote.'

When he made no move to swallow it she leant across and removed the cup from his hands to take a sip.

'See. Not poisonous. In fact, quite palatable.' She repressed a shiver as the aftertaste hit her and hoped that he had not seen it.

'Palatable?' He questioned when he had finished. 'You call that palatable?' A film of froth coated his upper lip before he licked it away. 'Come, Emma, and I will show you palatable.'

Once outside, he took a turning that she had not seen before that led to a conservatory almost entirely formed by glass, opening out to a wide and formal garden.

'My mother's contribution to the place,' he remarked as he saw her astonishment. 'It is a tradition that the Wellingham wives are always good at something. My grandmother was a horsewoman of great repute and my great-grandmother a musician. It is said at night through the corridors of the west wing that you can still hear the haunting tunes of her pianoforte.' He smiled. 'Ghosts are mandatory in a place like this, though I have never seen one.'

'What was Melanie good at?' The thought became a voiced question and she cursed as she saw his withdrawal.

'My wife was also good at music and good at being a wife,' he said simply and took the head off an orange chrysanthemum at his feet.

'She was beautiful.'

'Yes.'

'Is she the reason you do not sleep?'

He stood perfectly still. God, he seldom spoke of Melanie. And never to anyone save Taris. But here in the light of day, after a night when he hadn't had a moment's sleep, it was suddenly easy. Emma Seaton made it so.

'I was not at home when she died. I was not at home for her funeral. I should have been home.' He was astonished at the well of information he had given her and the depth of his anguish. If he had been by himself, he would have slammed his fist into something hard and finished off another bottle. But he wasn't alone.

'My brother also died when I was not with him. He was three.'

Asher looked up and focused. For the first time since he had met her, he felt as if he was actually hearing about someone in her family who had been real.

'I used to carry him everywhere, you see. I was six when he…went and acted his mother, I suppose. My name was the first one he ever spoke and I taught him songs in the dusk and rocked his hammock. He had a lisp. I remember that more now than his face.'

'How did he die?' She did not answer, though her paleness told him it had not been an easy death. He was trying to work out what lesson he could take from her confidence when she began to speak again.

'How long ago was it that your wife died?'

'Three years.'

'People used to say to me "time softens pain." And I used to think nothing will ever soften this ache. Nothing. But time did. It flattened out the rawness and left only memories. Good memories. Now when I think of James—that was his name—I think of his lisp and his curly blond hair and the thoughts make me smile.'

'I rarely speak of Melanie to anyone.'

'But you should, for it helps. A worry shared is a worry halved. Have you not heard the old adage?'

'Your father again?'

She smiled and in the light of the new day her dimples were as easy to see as the faint holes in her ears. For earrings, he determined, and not just one, either. A whole row of tiny marks pierced both lobes. He imagined jewels sparkling there and was still as a memory shifted and was lost.

Reaching out, he touched the slight indentations and she didn't stop him. Rather she leaned into his embrace.

She was so damnably responsive, he thought. Any slight caress had her heart beating faster and the flush well upon her cheeks. What would it be like to part the moist lips of her womanhood and slip inside? The thought had him stiffening and he pulled away.

Hell. After yesterday's débâcle he was back to acting like some green boy straight out of school. He wondered if she would notice the thickening bulge at the front of his trousers. His much-too-tight trousers, he amended, and readjusted them for the second time in two days.

The sound of his mother's voice made him groan. To be caught in the gardens by a parent with his trousers metaphorically down was something he had not contemplated. It hadn't happened at seventeen, so he had certainly not expected it to happen at thirty-one. Pulling the front of his long jacket closed he watched as Alice Wellingham, the Dowager Duchess of Carisbrook, was wheeled into the gardens by her maid. A quick look at Emma Seaton disorientated him. She was staring straight at him and trying not to smile. Lord, he thought. He was being given the run around by a Catholic chit, who had fed him a potion of ingredients that were causing his eyes to blur with tiredness.

His mother's smile was not helping either. He recognised that look, had seen it before every time some eligible woman had come into the sphere of his notice since the death of his wife, but today for the first time he was unreasonably irritated by it.

'You look terrible, Asher.'

'Good morning, Mother.'

'You look terrible and your servants let it slip that you have not slept at all in a week. And you have finished as many bottles of brandy as you do usually in a month.' Her voice broke. 'You will kill yourself with this behaviour and I hate to think what might happen to Falder and the dukedom.'

'Taris would undoubtedly assume the mantle of responsibility were such an unlikely event to occur.' He was cruel in his response, but he had had this talk before and did not want it in front of Emma Seaton now.

'Unlikely?' His mother was about to say more when her eyes rested on the face of Emerald and he introduced her.

'You are the Countess of Haversham's niece, are you not?'

'I am.'

'Many years ago I had a passing acquaintance with her family. Which branch do you hail from?'

'A distant one, I am afraid.'

Emma was a master at not answering any question about her past, Asher thought, but his mother failed to note the fact.

'She had a brother, Beauvedere. Have you ever come across him?'

'I do not believe so.'

'Then it is well that you haven't—I often wonder what happened to him. He was a striking man with the bluest eyes and a way with the women that was legendary. Ashborne always said he would come to no good…' She began to giggle. 'I am sorry. It is age, I think, this constant referral to times past. Easy to remember what happened thirty years ago and hard to think what it was one did yesterday. Instead of regaling you with old nonsense, I should be asking if are you being properly looked after here at Falder. Do you like the room you've been given? You are in the yellow room are you not? Do you play whist?'

'Badly.' Emerald looked startled by the quick changes of topic.

'Good. Then I shall set you up as my opponent this evening. Would you mind? My sister usually partners me, but she has gone down to London for the week as my nephew has arrived from the Americas. You will have a lot to catch up on, Asher,' she added, and even as she said the words his heart sank.

Just another person to tell him how he had changed for the worse.

He hoped that his cousin would keep any criticisms to himself and was suddenly as tired by it all as he ever had been.

It was the potency of Emma's remedy combined with a lack of sleep, he determined, and resolved to knock himself out early tonight with a strong brandy. He hoped belatedly that no maid had woken his brother slumbering on the armchair in front of Melanie's portrait. Taris must have come back into the room. He frowned. He had not heard him do so, which in turn suggested that some time around the very early dawn he had, after all, nodded off. The notion cheered him considerably. If he could sleep a little, it would follow that he could also sleep a lot. As his mother's maid wheeled her from the garden, he had another thought.

'Does the potion you made act as a sort of sleeping draught?' He could barely keep his eyes open.

'It does. And quite quickly too.' The laugh she ended the sentence with worried him.

'How quickly?'

When the dizzy whorl hit him he had his answer, then he felt only blackness.

He slept twenty hours straight and awakened just as the sun was rising on the dawn of the following day.

Emma Seaton sat next to him, reading Mary Wollstonecraft, the revolutionary tract criticising the restricted educative norms for women. Even her reading matter worried him.

'You are awake?' she said softly and put down the book. 'I know that I should not be here, but it was my potion and I was worried that perhaps I had wrongly remembered the proportions. I came in to see that you still breathed.'

'Just here?' he asked back and looked around the room for any signs of shifted possessions.

'I would not hurt your family. I like them.'

'But you would hurt me?' He was suddenly still, for today everything seemed clearer. It was him she had bumped into at Jack's ball and him she had targeted at the Bishop's dinner. Talking with George about it the next day, he had discovered that Lady Emma Seaton had intimated to Flora that she was an old friend of his and that she should be pleased to renew the acquaintance.

And when she had fallen against him at the ball he had known her faint to be false.

Lying on his back in bed with almost nothing on, however, he felt it was neither the time nor the place for confrontation. Consequently he turned the subject.

'You could probably make a fortune curing the plight of London's insomniacs with your tonic. The *ton* would take to you like a saviour.'

'How do you feel?'

'Better.'

'You do not sound it.'

'How do I sound?'

'Annoyed.'

'And you could not imagine why?'

'I gave you the gift of sleep.'

'You knocked me out and God knows what you have been up to in the meantime, making free with the things in my house in your quest for…what?' Steely eyes swept across her. 'Is it money? You look as if you might need some.'

Today he was like a bear with a sore head.

'My clothes may not be the latest vogue in London, but I assure you that it is from lack of desire rather than from lack of funds.'

'You would not want a new gown?'

'I know that to you the idea may be a preposterous one, but not all women have the need to garb them-selves in the very latest style. Some—like me, for example—would rather buy books.'

He began to laugh. 'Use my library, then. Feel free to choose something other than Wollstonecraft.'

He looked immeasurably younger with the humour dancing in his eyes and she capitulated. 'When you feel better later on in the day, perhaps we might enjoy a discussion on the relative merits of women's rights.'

'Perhaps,' he murmured and pulled a pillow over his head, ending any possibility of conversation.

Chapter Eight

Emerald walked to the sea early before anyone was about, before the night stars had faded from the sky, before the chamber maids had risen from their beds, and before Miriam would have the notion to miss her and comment. She had searched Falder for hours last night, searched Asher's room and the alcoves off it, searched the kitchens and the salons and the library. Searched the map room that Miriam had spoken of and come away with nothing. Had he thrown the cane away? She shook her head. The jewels on the carved head were too valuable to just get rid of and even the most dull-witted of folk could have determined the worth of the thing. Had he sold it off? Could she ask him somehow of its whereabouts without raising his curiosity and jogging his memory?

The water was cold as she waded into it, but not the freezing cold she had expected and the temperature took her thoughts on to further possibilities.

Looking around, she wondered if she dared to take off her gown and swim out to the first break of the waves. Behind her the land was silent and grey, a row of tall dark pines sheltering the beach from a cottage that lay half a mile in from where she stood, and the cove was bound at both ends by sharp outcrops of rock. No access there, then. No sudden stranger. No peeping Toms or vagrant passers-by.

She made her mind up in a moment and walked to a large bush at the head of the beach, shrugging off her jacket and her gown and boots. She left her silk gloves on. Out of habit. The slight breeze sent goose-bumps across the skin on her forearms and she laughed in sheer and unadulterated joy. Freedom.

Her first true freedom in four months. She rubbed away the tears that started in her eyes and walked straight into the ocean.

Asher saw her from a distance, a lonely Aphrodite with her hair a froth of bright gilt curls upon her head. Nothing was hidden. Nothing. Her long slender legs and arms, her rounded bottom, her waist, her full breasts moving up and down as she turned to look at the shore one last time before diving under. And under. And under…

His heart began to race and he urged his mount on, hitting the beach in a flat-out gallop and pulling off his boots and jacket after he had dismounted. God, where the hell was she?

'Emma.' His voice was wild, angry, desperate,

furious, the beat of his heart so loud he thought he might fall over with the power of the blood racing through his veins, thought he might explode with the red-hot fear, thought he might…

She came up fifty yards further out from where he had last seen her and it was her laughter that sent him completely over the edge, a laughter that stopped abruptly as she turned and her eyes caught his own.

'Get out of the water. Now.' He could do nothing to soften his wrath. All he wanted was for her to be safe.

'Go back.' Her voice was breathless, horrified. 'Go away. I do not need any help.' Turquoise eyes searched the shore for any sign of others and her cheeks, despite the cold of the sea, were a burning bright hot red.

He was not swayed at all. 'If you don't come out this second, I'll come in and get you.'

Emerald bobbed down in the water and wondered what to do now, for Asher Wellingham stood directly in a line in front of her clothes. From the look on his face she didn't think he'd be making anything easy for her either.

Already the water had lapped at his trousers and was now just above the point of his knees. Would he keep coming? Would he swim in and drag her out as he threatened?

'All right, then. Turn around.' Her placatory tone was hardly won, and when she saw the white of his teeth gleam in a quick smile she was pressed not to call his bluff and see just who was the stronger swimmer. But where could she then come ashore?

'Turn around.' She repeated the command when he made no move to do so and her trepidation grew as a movement on the high ground behind Asher formed the shape of another man, far away enough to still be safe, but coming closer with each wasted second. Her distraction had Asher turning.

'It's Malcolm Howard, a cottar from the hill.' His barely concealed laughter made her swear and, swimming in on the first wave, she stood up as late as she could manage it. Asher Carisbrook held his bulky jacket out to her, but not before he had had a good eyeful.

'Most gentlemen would have at least averted their faces,' she ground out and pulled her hand away, shrugging into his jacket with the intent of showing as little flesh as possible and pleased when the hem fell below her knees.

'Most ladies would have worn a shift,' he returned, looking over his shoulder and whistling. His large black stallion walked from the bushes at the top of the beach, carefully picking his way across the sand. Glancing across his shoulder, Emerald was surprised to see no sign of the stranger in the distance.

'Malcolm generally calls in at his brother's cottage. It's just behind that hillock,' he added with an edge of humour in his words.

'And you knew that?'

'I did.'

No repentance. No apology. No remorse. But the light in his eyes had changed. Pulling on his boots, he

The Harlequin Reader Service — Here's how it works:

Accepting your 2 free books and 2 free mystery gifts places you under no obligation to buy anything. You may keep the books and gifts and return the shipping statement marked "cancel". If you do not cancel, about a month later we'll send you 6 additional books and bill you just $4.94 each in the U.S. or $5.49 each in Canada, plus 25¢ shipping & handling per book and applicable taxes if any.* That's the complete price and — compared to cover prices of $5.99 each in the U.S. and $6.99 each in Canada — it's quite a bargain! You may cancel at any time; but if you choose to continue, every month we'll send you 6 more books, which you may either purchase at the discount price or return to us and cancel your subscription.

*Terms and prices subject to change without notice. Sales tax applicable in N.Y. Canadian residents will be charged applicable provincial taxes and GST. All orders subject to approval. Credit or debit balances in a customer's account(s) may be offset by any other outstanding balance owed by or to the customer. Please allow 4 to 6 weeks for delivery. Offer available while quantities last.

If offer card is missing write to: The Harlequin Reader Service, 3010 Walden Ave., P.O. Box 1867, Buffalo, NY 14240-1867

BUSINESS REPLY MAIL
FIRST-CLASS MAIL   PERMIT NO. 717   BUFFALO, NY

POSTAGE WILL BE PAID BY ADDRESSEE

HARLEQUIN READER SERVICE
3010 WALDEN AVE
PO BOX 1867
BUFFALO NY 14240-9952

NO POSTAGE
NECESSARY
IF MAILED
IN THE
UNITED STATES

mounted his horse with one quick movement and held out his right hand.

'Come, Emma, I will take you home.'

With sand on her feet and slick with seawater, she was hoisted up before she could argue and the warmth of his body made her start. She leant forward, hot with chagrin and flushed with something else much less definable.

'There is a hay barn in a paddock over the hill. We'll get your clothes and you can change there.'

'With you watching?'

His bark of laughter was contagious and she hid a smile as they rode. Dressed in nothing more than a too-big jacket and miles away from anyone or anywhere, she still felt safe. Asher Wellingham always made her feel safe.

'Where did you learn to swim?'

'In Jamaica.' The petulant silence she had meant to maintain seemed childish and stupid in the face of his humour.

'Sure as hell your father did not teach you.'

'No, it was a servant who showed me.'

'Dressed in more than you are now, I should hope.'

'It was hot and I was a child.'

'And now you are most definitely a woman.'

His free arm skimmed down across the side of her thigh and her breath stopped. 'Are you an innocent, Emma?'

'I beg your pardon?' She could barely believe that he could have asked her such a question.

'An innocent. A woman who has not had the pleasure yet of being with a man. If you are, then I should beg your forgiveness for even suggesting it, but if you are not, then you might entertain the notion of a dalliance that could be of benefit to both of us.'

'A dalliance?'

He pushed forward and she felt the hard ridge of his manhood against the small of her back.

'You want something of me and I want something of you. Badly. Perhaps we could accommodate each other and both come out the happier for it.'

His words tickled her neck and, with the hot flesh of the horse beneath her bottom and Asher Wellingham at her back, Emerald felt like simply leaning back and falling into his dangerous promise. Jamaica had hardly been a world where the passions between a man and a woman were hidden and the morality that hampered just about every social exchange here would have been deemed ludicrous there.

Say yes, her body screamed. No ties. No promises. Just the simple act of union. Here in the barn. Now.

Another voice countered the first one. The sensible voice of a woman who had been around men all her life and knew the easy empty promises they made when the bloodlust consumed them.

He was a duke, for goodness' sake, and his suggestion was that of a man who was used to women saying yes. Such men did not offer more to one whom they suspected of being a thief. She had seen Asher Wellingham in the ballrooms of London, seen the hooded glances of a hundred women with more impeccable credentials than she had. A richer family. A fairer face. Titles of equal standing to his own. And that was before she even considered their shared past.

Her eyes fell on his left hand as she shook her head. She noticed the knuckles whiten around the reins and a small voice inside her wished that he might just reach over and take what he had not been offered, a complete abnegation of any decision on her behalf. But he didn't. The gentleman in him, she mused.

'I have never—' She broke off. Horrified. What had she been going to tell him? That she was a virgin? That she had never lain with any man before? Given her behaviour of late, she was certain he would not have believed her.

'Never?' The golden chips in his eyes darkened. 'I don't usually accost women so blatantly and I—' He halted in mid-sentence as he pulled on the bridle and, dismounting, walked the horse towards a barn perched in the trees.

Accost. Such a harsh word for what he had offered, she thought. And telling. An interpretation of motive? 'I will wait here while you change.' He used the briefest of contact to help her down from the horse.

Formal. Proper. A definitive shift from the suggestion he had just voiced. Clutching her clothes, she scurried into the building, angry at herself for caring.

An easy lay and an easy leave. She remembered her father talking of the women he had bedded and left. Heartened by the memory, she bit back further introspection and finished dressing, tying the laces on her boots with hands that shook. Damn it. Why was it that she became a wanton in the company of Asher Wellingham? She thought of his glance ranging across her naked body and shivered. What had he thought? The butterfly on her breast had been plainly visible, as had the long curling scar across her right thigh. She had seen the surprise on his face when he had offered the jacket.

Surprise, speculation and lust.

Taking a breath, she walked outside. He stood with his back to the barn. Jacketless and shirt open, his dark hair fell across his collar, long from behind and slightly curly, the fabric of his shirt outlining well-defined muscle. Not a sedentary man, she mused. When he turned, she saw in his eyes that which she imagined must be reflected in her own.

Wariness.

'Thank you for your jacket.' Traces of seawater darkened the light brown fabric as he slung it carelessly across the pommel of his saddle.

'You are welcome.'

The English distance in his voice made her wince. In Jamaica, difficulties had always been settled through argument. So eminently practicable, everything said and no chance of ambiguity. Here, problems simmered beneath a more polite façade, the bubbling undercurrent of dispute left unsolved and unspoken; as he offered to help her mount, she wished that he might ask her again to consider this *dalliance* with at least a semblance of love in his eyes.

The very thought made her heart race. 'I shall walk home from here, your Grace, for it is an easy stroll.'

Nothing would make her climb on to his horse again and feel his thighs next to hers and his breath on her neck. Nothing.

He bowed his head slightly and dug his heels into the flanks of his big black stallion, gone before she had the nerve to call him back.

Signalling Azziz with her candle at midnight Emerald joined him on the road that swung between Falder and the sea. He did not look pleased.

'Have you bedded him?'

'Have I what?' Even in the darkness she knew he must see the mounting blush on her cheeks at his question.

'Bedded him? Toro said he saw you leave the water today in the company of Asher Wellingham. He said you were naked.'

'I'd been for a swim. He found me there.'

'I will kill him.'

Laying her hand upon his sleeve, she pulled him back. 'It was my fault. I should not have gone in without clothes and he did not touch me. He was a gentleman in all of his actions.' She mentioned neither Asher's suggested dalliance nor the barn to him.

'Put a knife to Carisbrook's throat tonight, Emmie, and demand the parchment. Then we can run for the coast and take sail to Jamaica. If we delay our leave much longer, we'll have no money for the passage home.'

The brutal thrust of Azziz's argument worried her. Even a month ago she might have suggested the same thing, but now…

'I'll sell my pearls. That should tide us over for at least a while.'

Azziz shook his head. 'They are the only thing of your mother's you have left. You always said you'd never be parted from them.'

'Please, Azziz, have Toro take the pearls down to London and find the best jeweller in town. You know where they are hidden in Miriam's house. Just give me another few days.'

Another few days. Another caress? Another chance?

She shook her head to rid herself of the image of Asher on the horse behind her and felt the hairs on her arms rise up in memory.

'I could rob a wealthy traveller. It should be enough.'

'No.' Horror swamped her. 'Not in England. Here you are hanged for such an offence. Far better to sell the pearls and buy us some time.'

'If you let me at Carisbrook for an hour—'

'No.'

'His sister, then. Word has it they are close.'

'Leave the family alone. I mean it.'

'Lord, you were always headstrong. Beau had more faults than any one man had a right to, but he was your father and Carisbrook killed him in cold blood.'

'Cold blood? A mid-ocean encounter between two warring ships.'

'You would excuse this English duke?'

She turned away and looked back towards Falder. From here the lights of the house showed bright against the hills behind it. 'My father lived by the sword just as surely as he died by it and before I came here I thought that Asher Wellingham was of the same ilk. But now? I think he is as honourable as you are and I would not see him hurt.' She swallowed as she felt Azziz's large hand come to rest upon her shoulder.

'You like him, don't you, girl?' His voice was soft. 'How do you think he would react if he knew of your Sandford blood?'

'Badly.' Her response was as honest as the question asked.

'And if he exposes you, there will be little that anyone could do to stem the damage. Trust him and you could well be as dead as your father and what will happen, then, to Miriam and Ruby? If you will not think of yourself, at least think of them.'

Emerald shivered. For the very first time in all of her life she had met a man who made her feel like a woman. A man who made her imagine things that she had not before even considered.

Naked beneath his jacket and walking into the barn, a part of her had wanted him to follow her in and take away her virginity. She was twenty-one and she had never bedded a man. It was time. It was beyond time. The throb of lust deep within her loins surprised her and she was pleased when Azziz left his warnings at that and turned towards the line of trees that ran across the eastern ridge and away from Falder.

* * *

In the moonlight the garrets and turrets of the house were light against the sky and, skirting the pebble-chip pathways beyond the gardens, she saw a silhouette in the bay window. Stopping, she retraced her steps and crept through the undergrowth directly in line with the uncurtained window.

Asher stood against the glass, looking out. Behind him, hovering in the alcove, was the painted image of his long-dead wife. Watching him. Tying him to a sadness that was all consuming and never ending. She could so often see that wounded look in his eyes, like a man who bled from a gash he could not find and had ceased to notice his own hurt.

Melanie Wellingham, the dead Duchess of Carisbrook.

Everything had to do with her and with his broken hand and his blind brother. And it was all intertwined with Falder, a thousand years of history bearing down hard upon his shoulders. She started forward and stopped. What could she say?

Kiss me. Love me. Let me stay here. Here. For ever. Where the names of your ancestors march through the centuries and the shivers of memory are kind.

Kinder than my own memories. Much kinder.

A ship in the midst of an angry sea and the promise of another storm chasing hard on the heels of the first one. The English ship with the promise of well-laden hulls and Asher Wellingham waiting, sword in hand, on his quarterdeck with two dozen men behind him. An easy target. Slow. Cumbersome. The lightning off the sea silhouetting everything.

She had felt his focus and his expertise, but had still been surprised as he had swung through a swathe of sailors to reach her father. It was the whine of a cannonball that threw him into her path, and into the radius of her blade, though he had laughed as her sword crossed his own. 'You have chosen the wrong pathway, lad. Throw in with me and I will see that you have safe passage back to England—you are too young to be losing your life to the likes of this motley crew.'

Grasping her sword tighter, she had fended him off, though his proficiency was a revelation. He had been playing with her. The realisation had come with a great rush of amazement, given her own ability at swordplay, and she had been pleased to see the amusement harden as she had cut across his left sleeve and drawn blood. If she was going to die, she had wanted it to matter, though his sudden feint had her fighting arm pinioned against the mizzenmast.

'Drop the sword and I will spare you. It's not my way to slaughter innocents.'

His breath had mingled with her own and it was then that their eyes truly caught.

Tight and close.

'Lord, you're a girl.' Amazement narrowed his eyes as he brought his hand across the quivering fullness of her lips. Even now through the gathering years of time Emerald could still feel that caress, still feel the way her body had simply melted into heat.

Unexpectedly sweet. Undeniably woman. In the middle of an ocean, in the middle of a battle, she had run her tongue across the saltiness of his thumb and shock had claimed them both.

She had seen it in the shards of his eyes, the paler ring of brown flaring golden. And she had felt it in the sudden rush of blood beating in her throat, though her father's shout had broken the spell as he advanced upon them, murder in his eyes. In a quick protection she had rammed the hilt of her sword hard across Asher Wellingham's temple and upended him into the sea. A chance at least to cheat death. Ten summers of sailing with Beau had at least taught her that.

'Lord,' she said aloud and banished such memory, running her hands across the knife tucked into her belt.

Right. Wrong.

Good. Bad.

Aboard the *Mariposa* she had been her father's daughter. But here she was no longer sure of anything at all.

'Asher.' She whispered his name and held her fingers up against the warmth of sound.

A home. A family. Responsibilities. Accountability. Unlike her father, the Duke of Carisbrook took these things seriously and she admired him for it, the questionable morality they had lived by in Jamaica less certain here.

Stepping back into the shadows, she cursed her father and headed to the sanctuary of her room.

* * *

Asher paced up and down and remembered the sight of Emma Seaton coming unclothed towards him, the water slick upon her body and the sand marking her feet.

She was the most beautiful woman he had ever seen.

His eyes flicked to the painting of his wife in the small alcove and for the first time he found it difficult to remember her face in life. The exact colour of her eyes, the sharp line beneath the bridge of her nose.

Instead the image of Emma Seaton walking from the water towards him kept replaying in his mind, the butterfly tattoo as surprising as the deep curling scar upon her right thigh. He had enough wounds on his own body to know the mark of a sword when he saw one.

Where had she got it? When had she got it? And why, despite taking everything else off, had she not removed her gloves? What was she hiding there?

He began to smile as he lifted a glass of water to his lips.

Water?

Today even his choice of beverage was different. Emma Seaton made him different. More alive. She made the very air of Falder ring with a vibrancy long missing.

And what might have happened had he followed her into the barn? He would have taken her hard and fast without a care for who was around or what the consequences might have been. She did that to him with her sun-browned skin and her turquoise eyes. Made him careless and reckless. Brought out the man he used to be. The man who had loved and risked and lost.

Lord. What the hell was happening to him? He had

to stop it, for she was dangerous to everything he had made himself believe in.

Rules. Regularity. Carefulness. Control.

In chaos came loss. Of all the men in the world, he should be the best to know it.

He flicked open the casement of his timepiece.

Four o'clock. Outside the wind was mounting and the quarter-moon was high. He glanced down at the atlas in front of him and traced his fingers across the ragged outline of Jamaica. Emma's home. The place where she had been formed. His eyes wandered further west into the shoals of the Yucatan Channel.

His ship had come through the mist there on to the Sandford vessel with remarkable speed and silence and no trick of intent, either, just the cold hard slice of revenge and then an ending. He thought he would have felt more than he did as he had run Beau Sandford through the guts with the sharp point of his sword. But he hadn't. God. After a year of captivity and another year to recover, he should have allowed himself to feel more. He stretched out his right hand and swore, the stumps of his missing fingers outlined against the light of the lamp. Even now the hate still festered.

Looking at the reflection of himself in the window, he frowned. He had been so certain of his course in life until lately… Lately, the sharp focus had dimmed and another reality had brightened.

Emma. She was taking up all his waking thoughts and sliding into his dreams. Effortlessly.

And he could not let her with her mystery and

secrets. Balling his right fist, he closed his eyes. The only way to protect himself was to never feel again.

Emma Seaton would be at Falder for three more days and then she would be gone. He resolved to spend as many of those as he could well away from her.

Chapter Nine

They tiptoed around one another at breakfast the next morning with polite smiles and bland words.

'Is the food to your satisfaction?'

'Would you mind passing the strawberry jam?'

And beneath it all ran an undercurrent of mounting desperation.

Emerald was glad Taris and Lucy were both at the table.

'I saw Malcolm Howard yesterday at the Red Lion. He said you had been swimming, Asher, down in Charlton Bay.'

'I took Artemis for a jog along the sand. Perhaps it was that he meant.' His voice and eyes gave absolutely nothing away as he reached across the table to help himself to some toast.

Taris changed his tack. 'Do you swim, Emma?'

'She does,' Asher answered for her, brown eyes flinting a warning, and Lucy, who caught neither the amusement of one brother nor the irritation of the other, jumped into the fray.

'Then you absolutely must teach me, for I have always longed to swim. What do you wear in the water?'

Emerald flushed deep red at the question and bent to cut up the omelette on her plate. 'The temperature of the water in England is a lot colder than that of Jamaica. If I were to venture in here, it would be merely a case of testing the water to the ankles,' she said finally when she had her heartbeat in some sort of check. She did not dare to chance a look at Asher.

Lies were one thing when the recipient had no notion of their falseness or otherwise. But Asher had been there. He had seen her, touched her, run his fingers across the bare skin at her shoulder… The heat in her cheeks did not abate and she took in several breaths to at least try to calm herself.

Damn it. She barely recognised this shrinking violet she had suddenly become and Lucy's puzzled frown only added to her discomfort. Suddenly the day stretching before her seemed indeterminably long. When Asher rose from the table and pushed his chair back, she was glad for it.

'I will be in Rochcliffe till the evening, Taris, and if I stay the night I will send word. Ladies.' His glance barely encompassed her and then he was gone, striding darkly through the dining-room portal. The sun slanting in from a nearby window gave the black of his hair a bluish light and highlighted the hard planes of his face.

* * *

She was in her bed by the window by ten o'clock that evening after spending an hour or so in the library with Taris, playing chess. Asher's absence had been a godsend, for under the simple pretext of exploring Falder further she had used the afternoon to search for any sign of her father's cane. And come away with nothing. Lord, she muttered to herself as she lay on her blankets and looked up at the sky, her time here was running out and, if she did not find the map soon, she had little chance of being invited back.

Where could he have hidden it? Where would she have hidden it?

If Falder had been a smaller home, everything would have been immeasurably less difficult, but with its numerous salons and bedchambers and nooks and crannies it was like a labyrinth, much of it joined through a series of inner passageways that defied reason.

Bolstering the pillows behind her back, she plucked her harmonica from beneath them and began to play, the gentle melody relaxing the strain of the day, and the tunes of Jamaica strangely comforting in the colder climes of Fleetness. Azziz had taught her the ways and whys of the instrument ten years ago on the slow watches of the *Mariposa* and ever since she had added songs to her repertoire that she could play by heart. Ruby had often sung along and danced to the music in the room they had shared off the Harbour Road in Kingston Town and the squalor of that time still haunted her: the danger, the lack of money, the dreadful yearning for the sea.

Here at Falder everything was easy and beautiful: the house, the furniture, the food and the people. A little money softened the rawness of life and a lot removed it completely. She smiled at her musings and then tensed as she heard footsteps in the corridor outside her room and a knock.

Tucking her hair back behind her ears and donning a nightrobe left in the wardrobe, she opened the door.

Asher stood there, wind-blown hair and drink-bruised eyes, the shadow of a twelve-hour stubble on his jaw. Carefully she edged the material of the sleeves down across her hands.

'I need to talk to you.'

'Here? Now?'

'It should only take a moment.'

'Very well.' She was not certain whether to invite him in or not. Granted, she knew enough about the social mores in England to also know that asking an unmarried man into your bedroom was unheard of. But did the rules apply when the same man was also the owner of the house? A refusal might look as if she imagined herself as feminine game or as if she suspected his intentions to be less than honourable. He solved the worry for her by staying on the threshold even as she gestured him to enter.

'No. I should not come in—' He stopped, clearly perturbed.

'Where did you get the tattoo? The butterfly.'

'Jamaica.'

'Is it normal there? Normal for the daughter of a devout father?'

'I think we both know the answer to that question,' she replied.

'I would like to hear it from you.'

'My father was not quite as you may imagine.'

'What exactly was he like, then?' His golden gaze flared in the candlelight.

'He was a man whom life had disappointed.' Pride kept her from saying more, and she was pleased when he changed the subject.

'Taris said that you are a fine chess player. It is not often that he loses. To anyone. Where did you learn?

'On the—' She stopped, horrified, as she realised what she had been about to say. *On the Mariposa.* Just like that.

'An uncle taught me,' she amended and held her breath as the awkwardness of the moment passed.

'I thought I heard music before, in here?'

'You did.' She brought the harmonica from her pocket and watched a range of emotions play across his face.

Puzzlement. Amusement. Interest.

'My family likes you, Lady Emma. Every time your name is mentioned, Taris and Lucinda sing your praises and it is not often that my brother waxes lyrical about anyone. Especially these days.'

'How did he lose his sight?' She asked the question quietly and was surprised by his sharp expression.

'An accident that should never have happened. If I

hadn't been—' He stopped and caught at control, the muscles on the line of his jaw quivering.

'I do not think he blames you, your Grace.'

He smiled at that and moved back. 'No, he doesn't.' Tight words rising from the depths of despair.

'But you blame yourself?'

Suddenly everything was crystal clear. His lack of help for Taris on the road to Thornfield. It was not anger at his affliction that held him back, but guilt. Guilt. The sheer knowledge of it made her insides weaken.

Such a complex man and so masculinely vulnerable. She swallowed back her pity, knowing that at this moment he would not want it, and, as if he could read her mind, he stepped away.

'We are due over at Longacres tomorrow for dinner with the Gravesons. After yesterday, if you would rather cancel, I would quite understand.'

'No, I would like to go.'

'If you could be ready at five, then we would be back before midnight.'

The noise of voices from the stairs that joined this floor to the next had him turning, and, drawing his coat against the draughts of cold in the passageway, he was gone.

She had nothing to wear and two hours to be ready to leave for the Gravesons. Grimacing she pulled the last of her dresses from its hanger. She had never been bothered before about the state of her clothes, but this gown was hardly salubrious wear for any occasion, let alone a dinner date with a duke. She would give anything for a dress that actually fitted her and had a colour in it that was neither pastel nor brown.

And her gloves? The grey silk pair she wore constantly was fraying not only at the wrist but at the base of one thumb now, and the seam was so narrow that she could not reunite the cloth without also altering the fit.

A knock at the door and Lucinda was in the room, her face falling as she glanced at the gown.

'Is this what you were planning to wear tonight? Perhaps I should warn you that Annabelle puts much stock in the dress sense of others.'

'Then she will be sorely disappointed with me, I fear.'

Lucy laughed. 'You do not enjoy fashion?' she asked at length.

'You sound like your brother.'

'Asher asked you about your gowns?'

'He did. And I told him that I would rather buy books.'

'And is that true?'

Emerald's telling hesitation brought Lucinda to her side. 'I knew that of course it would not be true.' She walked across to the wardrobe and firmly shut the door. 'Nothing in there will do, Emma. May I call you that?'

'My friends call me Emmie.'

'Then Emmie it is, and I have just the gown for you. It's in my room and it was one that my cousin left at Falder last year and she is about your size and colouring.'

'She wouldn't mind me using it?'

'No, not at all. She's the least fussy person I know and one of the nicest.'

* * *

An hour later Emerald barely recognised herself. She stood in front of a full-length mirror in Lucy's room and stared. This dress was the first one she had ever worn that actually nearly fitted her. Gone were the sagging bodices and the false hems. Gone were the short not-quite-fit-me sleeves and the hideously high or dangerously low necks.

But it was the colour that owed the most to the transformation. Deep midnight blue with a hint of silky grey on its edge, the fabric showed up the line of her body and the gold of her skin. In this she did not look insipid or washed out. In this her eyes were bright and her hair, carefully combed by a maid, was for the first time placed in some semblance of order. Even her ears looked different, for Lucy had found some topaz drops that had been her grandmother's.

'You look wonderful,' she said as she hooked the earrings in place. 'But you have more than one pierced hole?'

Emerald took in breath. 'It is the way in Jamaica.'

'And your gloves? Is it the way there to wear gloves all the time?'

Perfect blue eyes met her own.

'No. That is my choice. I like to wear them.'

'Then you should make it into a fashion statement.' Rattling around in her cupboard, Lucinda came up with some fine white lace elbow-length gloves, looking enquiringly at her when she did not remove her old ones.

There was little else to do but to peel off the grey pair. Quickly. She turned her palms upwards as she pulled the new ones on and took a peek at Asher's sister.

She had seen.

She knew it as soon as she looked.

'I burnt myself once.' It was all that she would admit. She was pleased to see the lace was lined in fine cream silk and that no trace of the reddened scar tissue could be seen. Flame left the sort of mark with its bone-deep ravages that made people turn their eyes away. And her hands had been on fire for all of a minute before she hit the sea.

'I would prefer that you said nothing of my scars to anyone.'

'I promise you I won't.' Lucy made much of folding away the discarded petticoats and chemises before asking quietly, 'Do they hurt?'

'No.'

Her mind ran backwards to a battle in the waters off Jamaica about a year after her first meeting with Asher Wellingham. Azziz had been behind her and Solly Connors out further under the yardarm. Morning fog had engulfed the *Mariposa* and the flash that came from nowhere was strangely magnified by the closeness. She remembered Solly's head flying past her, his body curled around the footrope as if his fingers had a mind of their own, the last ingrained act of survival imprinted in their being. And shouts from below as a fireball whirled up the mast and hit them, the main-course sheets soggy from the night-time rain shelter-

ing them from the sheer force of it. She had reached
out for the shroud and shifted her weight. But her
fingers did not grip, could not grip, and she had fallen,
fallen, fallen into the ocean.

When she woke up all hell had claimed her.

Thornfield came into view after a good fifteen
minutes in the carriage and Emerald was glad to see
it. Asher had hardly spoken to her and certainly had
not complimented her on the gown or her hair. Chagrin
was a strange emotion, she decided, a feminine art
form of guilt that she had always despised. But here
in the folding darkness of Fleetness Point she found
herself pouting at his negligence.

With a sigh she shifted position, bringing the
fullness of the skirt out from beneath her. Lucy had told
her to do so for the material was heavy silk and liable
to crush. In the dusk its silver shimmer was more noticeable, like a living moonbeam come to rest in her
dress. She absently shaded her fingers over the lightness and glanced at Asher Wellingham from the corner
of her eye.

He sat as far away from her as he could manage,
his hands tightly bound on his lap. Tonight he had
barely looked at her.

'I need to make a small detour to the harbour, for
my draughtsman in London is in need of some plans.'

Irritation dropped away to sheer delight.

'We will go aboard your ship?' She tried to make her
voice as indifferent as she could. But it was hard work.

'You can wait in the carriage, if you would rather. I will take just a moment to find the drawings and then we'll be on our way. Annabelle said six and it is not yet half past five, so there is still plenty of time.'

'I would be interested to go aboard.' She could not quite hide the excitement.

'Very well. Though I must warn you it is cramped and difficult to negotiate.'

'Difficult?' She opened her fan and hid a smile. 'I am sure I shall be able to manage, though I should not wish to be a nuisance…'

He did not answer as the carriage veered towards the harbour.

He helped her across the gangplank and the swell and ebb of the sea beneath her feet was like a caress.

Closing her eyes she savoured it, breathed it in.

'Are you all right?' There was urgency in his voice, and for the first time that night he touched her, his hand cupping her elbow as if to hold her up. She swayed into him, her body reacting before her mind warned her away.

'All right?' She was disorientated by sheer longing.

'Seasickness,' he clarified. 'It can sometimes hit quickly.'

'No, I am in good health.' With the greatest of will she broke the link between them and looked around, glad to feel her heart settling down to a more normal pace. 'It's a beautiful ship.' Her fingers reached out to the belayed halyard that led to the main lower topsail, so familiar she could have trimmed the sheet with her eyes closed.

'That's the rope that lets the sail drop. Without that we can't furl it.'

She smiled at his explanation, given to her in such simple terms. 'You have sailed a lot?'

'I used to.'

'But you don't any more?'

'I lost the taste for it,' he returned shortly and bade her follow him down the companionway. 'The chart-room is this way. Mind your step.'

It was the skirt, she thought later. In her haste she forgot to raise it properly and the toe of her shoe caught in the thick folds of silk and simply tipped her up. Asher caught her. Closer this time. The whisper of his breath touched her cheek and his hand fell across the swell of her bottom as he guided her to the master's cabin where they were cocooned in the quiet lap of the ocean, the smell of oil lamps mixing with the stronger scent of teak.

She felt the hard wooden ribs of the hull behind her back and the warm planes of his body at her front, pressing against her, closer. In the half-light only the snowy white of his cravat was plain. Everything else was melded into shadow.

'How do you do this?' he asked softly. 'How do you make me want you?' He raised her hand and the wet warmth of his tongue explored the space above the hem of her glove. And left her breathless.

'Asher.' She could barely say his name as her fingers

threaded through the length of his night-dark hair. She knew exactly what it was he spoke of, this want that defied all rationality and sense and delivered her to a place where nothing else mattered.

Just him. Her. Them.

With lips edged in anger his mouth took hers; when the hand that rested on her bottom firmed and guided her to the place between his legs, she groaned. It was the residue of yesterday's suggested dalliance, she was to think later and the conjured imaginings that she had dealt with as a result all through the previous night. She could not find it in her to say no, to place her hand on his and call a halt. No, rather she leaned into his embrace, pressed against his solidity as his fingers slid around the edge of her breast.

Here in the dark of the hold of his ship with the gentle sound of water on wood she had no words to stop him. Oh! Love came easy without the stinging drudge of memory, and the girl she had been in Jamaica was the woman who responded here.

Tell me.

Show me.

Take me.

'Emma, I want you.'

Emerald.

For the first time his use of a name not quite her own bothered her. His eyes were dark twin pools of intensity, the brown in them ringed with a harsher colour as he slipped the strap of her low-cut dress from her shoulder and bent his head. Flipping his tongue against her nipple once, he pulled back, watching the skin pucker and crinkle.

'At the dinner with the Bishop of Kingseat you did not wear undergarments and when you bent over…' He stopped, giving her the impression of a man only just holding on to some semblance of control. 'Suffice it to say that I have wanted to touch you here ever since then.' His thumb lightly skimmed the wet coldness of her nipple. 'And kiss you here.' His lips were warm against the small patch of freckles lying in her cleavage. 'I have wanted to know the taste of your sun-warmed skin and find the line where clothes have shielded you. His hand dipped lower. 'Have they, Emma? Shielded you? Here?'

She could not speak. She could only feel as hot drifts of longing assailed her and the rhythm of his breathing changed. Her eyes fell upon his lips. He had beautiful lips. Full and defined. The stubble on his jaw was light as her palm brushed against it and when he tipped her lips to his, the slick shattering passion spun her wild and heat took over.

Away. From everything. She was all woman. Open, alive, free. And he was the sun and the ocean and the warm solid earth.

Again.

For ever. Cast as she was from a storm into the safe harbour of his body. And needing refuge.

The heavy footfall of boots were suddenly heard above them on the deck.

'Hell.' He pulled away and helped her straighten herself, as a man came down the stairs.

'Duke, I thought I heard you…' The words petered out and stopped, uncertainty replacing the earlier hurry. 'I'm sorry.' The newcomer's voice held a strange quiver. Not sorry at all, she determined, but amused.

'This is Peter Drummond, an old friend of mine who is also the ship's captain. Peter, meet Lady Emma Seaton.'

'It is my pleasure,' he said softly, his glance falling to the crushed silk of her skirt. A definite question was in his eyes and the tone in his voice was puzzled.

'You got my note, then?'

'Note?' Asher shook his head.

'To meet here. I thought that was why…'

'I came for the plans to take up to London. Is there a problem?'

'There might be.'

Emerald could tell the man did not wish to say more in front of her, so excusing herself, she walked back up the steps and on to the moonlit deck. The quiet burr of voices from below was a backdrop to the frantic beat of her heart.

What had just happened? Again? If Peter Drummond had not come…?

She could not think of it. Did not want to think of it.

'I am the pirate's daughter,' she whispered to herself. *'The pirate's daughter. The pirate's daughter.'*

She remembered the taunts of the children on the dockside at Kingston Town, when the *Mariposa* had come into port, and the slanted glances of their parents.

Her father was a man who used fear to distance

himself from everyone. And he had never been honest. Just as she was not being honest. Here.

With Asher.

The realisation made her sick and when he rejoined her she was hard-pressed to smile. He seemed preoccupied and angry and threatening in a way he had not been ten minutes earlier. The evening sun made his hair darker, the tan of his face showing up his teeth and the velvet of his eyes.

He was beautiful.

She admitted this simple fact to herself. And smiled.

They had gone a good mile before he spoke and in a voice that sounded nothing like the one she had last heard him use.

'Who are the men camped in the wood?'

'I am not certain what you mean—' she began, but he interrupted her.

'The men you brought with you from Jamaica. Does that make my query any clearer?'

'Who told you that?'

'Peter Drummond just now and Tony Formison a few days ago. His father owns the ship you came on and he remembers you disembarking with a black man and an Arab, four chests of books and your hair a damn lot longer than it appears to be now.'

'I see.' There was no point in denying it, so she regrouped her defences and tried to look contrite. 'They are here to see that I am protected.'

'Protected against whom?' He had the answer

even as he asked it. She could see the flint of disbelief on his face.

'And if they caught us like now, alone? What would happen then?'

'I suppose they would have to kill you.'

He laughed and then cursed. 'What makes you so certain that they could?'

'You strike me as a man who could easily protect himself, but if there were two of them, then, perhaps—'

He didn't let her finish.

'Who exactly are they?'

'My servants,' she ventured. 'When I left Jamaica for England it would have been dangerous to travel alone. They offered to accompany me to London.'

'And then they offered to follow you up here?'

'Yes.' Even to her ears the explanation sounded implausible.

'And you did not think to ask me to house them at Falder, in the servants' quarters?'

'They like their independence. Once they saw I was safely at your house and that you were a gentleman—'

He interrupted her. 'How do you contact them?'

'By the signal of a candle at night.' She was honest in her answer, for he looked as if another lie might well incite his anger.

'Through the window of your room?'

'Yes.'

'And should I worry that they may frisk Falder with even more competence than you have?'

Because his summation of the situation was so close

Another convert to the cause of Emma Seaton, Asher thought. Lucy. Taris. And now Mrs Wilson.

He took a breath and addressed his housekeeper. 'Lady Emma Seaton will not be back.'

'Oh, dear, your Grace. Well, all as I can say is that it's a shame, it is, for a nicer guest we have not had, or a tidier one. And what should I do with all the shells that she collected?'

Asher began to laugh even as he stood.

Five minutes later he took to the stairs leading to Emma's room and opened the wide oak door.

A nest of blankets sat near the French doors, the sheets folded on the bed in a neat pile. And unused, as was the thick felted quilt.

Emma Seaton travelled light and rough, he thought and crossed to the balcony. Two heavy chairs had been moved and placed together to form a platform that one might stand upon. With care he mounted them and before him, through the green fold of a hillock, lay the sea.

The sea.

If he closed his eyes, he could hear it, as she must have done. My God, every single thing he ever found out about her confused him. She was not used to sleeping in a bed and she liked the sea. And the only thing in this room that had been used while she inhabited it was a candle.

A candle used to signal her men in the wood in the very dead of night. A candle used to search his home.

He ran his fingers through his hair and wished she were still here.

Near him. Safe. And then he cursed himself for thinking it.

It was late when Asher and Taris and Lucinda arrived back in London, and Jack Henshaw, who had been waiting for them at Carisbrook House, had worrying news.

'The Countess of Haversham is ill and Lady Emma has sent away the doctor and taken full charge of the situation herself. Unusual, but dutiful,' he added and leant forward to his drink. 'Gregory Thomas, the physician, is an acquaintance of mine. He said he saw the Countess last in the company of a burly black man lighting a sweet-smelling fire of oil in a copper basin while the niece pushed hot pins into the side of her aunt's neck. Many are saying it to be witchcraft.'

Asher swore. Lord, if that was the case, Emma was going to be sore pressed to re-enter the narrow world of society. Clothes a little odd or outdated were one thing, but it was quite another to be accused of practising sorcery. And so blatantly. 'Why the devil would she have done that? Why would she be negligent with her reputation?' The answer came to him immediately.

Because Emma Seaton did not mean to stay in England at all. Because the search of Falder was a means to an end and that end was to be once again ensconced in the place she called home. Jamaica.

When Jack left Taris lingered and Asher could tell that he was disturbed by something, though as his brother began speaking the subject was very different from that which he had expected.

'If you have an Achilles' heel, Asher, it is your love of control.'

'You're speaking of Emma Seaton, I presume?' he bit back. Tonight he was tired.

'She is not like the other women here. She is strong and independent and would not thank you, I think, for seeing to her reputation.'

'You do not think I should help her?' Real anger reverberated in his question.

'I do not think that you should judge her by the standards of society.'

'Because she so obviously is from somewhere else?'

'No. Because she is very much her own person. Like I am mine. Sometimes, even despite my lack of sight, I can feel you watching me and worrying about the next person with too loud a voice who will inadvertently hurt my feelings.' He laughed and softened his tone. 'What will you do, Asher? Fight them all because you feel responsible? Don't you see? I came to the Caribbean to find you on my own accord and Emma Seaton has come to London on her own accord. It is not you who needs to calm the waters to make sure that she fits. She doesn't and she probably doesn't want to either.'

Asher slapped his hand against the wood in the wall. Hard. 'And where will she fit, then? Jamaica has hardly nurtured and protected her.'

Taris laughed. 'Lord, Asher. It's more than a feeling of responsibility for her, isn't it?'

Turning away, he mulled over his brother's last question and was glad when he did not demand an answer, but left the room in that particular way he had of moving around objects.

More than responsibility?

More than friendship?

For a moment Asher imagined Emma Seaton as the Duchess of Carisbrook, immune against all criticism just because of who he was. He could protect her. From everyone.

But would she want him to?

Without a doubt he knew that she wouldn't.

'Lord help me,' he muttered and was wondering what the hell he was going to do when his eyes fell on a cane near the door. Uneasy conjecture caught as he remembered the conversation in the coach on the way home from Longacres. Canes. Questions. The quick flare of interest.

In the corner of a room off the blue salon was a stand set in the wall, hidden behind the thick fold of a velvet curtain. Two canes sat inside it and, as his fingers reached for the black-and-ivory stick studded in jewels, memory turned.

He'd taken this from the *Mariposa* after he'd returned to the Caribbean and killed Sandford. A crutch to aid his damaged leg. Could this be what Emma was after? The stones were valuable after all, and it was a fine piece of carving. Intrigued, he examined it closely and noticed that the handle was not quite round, the ornate twists of wood hiding a catch beneath the lip of ebony stones. Perhaps she had been interested in this particular cane not for its value, but for something else! Something hidden. Swearing, he ran his nail across a ridge and shaved off parings of wax, the sealant hindering the downward motion of the clasp. A dull click and the handle parted company with the body of the wood, a hollowed compartment inside becoming plainly visible.

He smiled at the ridiculous ease of it all as he ironed out a parchment under the light.

A map, he determined. An old map of the Eleutheran inlets and with much more than the gauge of depth shown. A map delineating caves of gold! Contemplation sparked discomfort. What would a woman like Lady Emma Seaton want with such a map and how could she have known about it?

Slipping the parchment into a secret drawer in his desk he sat down to write a note.

The noise came later, much later, as he sat in the darkened library before the embers of a dying fire. A small scratching at first and then a larger bang. Someone was in his office down the hall.

Emma? His heartbeat surged as he moved forward into the passageway that divided the rooms. When the heavy wood of a baton hit him square across his shoulders and sent him to the floor, the parquet was cold beneath his cheek. For a moment he felt winded by shock and disorientated.

'Where's the bloody map?' the larger one of the two men demanded, his accent somewhat similar to Emma's. The lilt of an island cadence. Lord, were these her men, tired of the more gentle persuasion? Dizziness dissipated under the larger threat to his life and, surging forward, he knocked the man nearest to him off his feet. The sharp blade of a knife nicked the flesh of his upper arm, and, swearing, Asher lurched to standing and eyed them both warily, the circling distance between adversaries lessening.

'Who the hell are you?' He looked down at his hand. A red tide of blood dripped from his fingers. The damned blade had got an artery, he thought, suddenly light-headed, though he shook his head to dispel the gathering haze and held his wounded arm tight against his body, balancing as he calculated the seconds left before they rushed him.

They came together and the remembered moves of fighting learned in the hot compound of the Caribbean returned to him. Effortlessly. The sharp clean noise of a broken bone and a knife falling to the floor, to a quick curse of anger as his assailant's heads met.

'Who the hell are you?' he bellowed again as the second thief rose uncertainly up. He had no more energy to fight, though already he could hear the running footsteps of those in the house. Evidently the other man heard it too. He grabbed his accomplice around the shoulders and they crossed to the window and were outside even as he slid to the floor.

Asher looked up as Taris, Lucinda and four servants

entered the room. 'Get a doctor,' he said as spurts of his blood rose into the air before him.

He came to in his bed. His sister sat beside him and he could see that she had been weeping. Taris watched him from the window and for a moment the world lightened and his ears hummed. Then it refocused, but strangely. He had never felt so tired in all of his life.

'What happened?' Even words were hard to say.

'You nearly bled to death, Asher, and would have done so had not Lady Emma turned up at the exact same moment that this all happened.' Taris spoke carefully.

'Emma?'

'She arrived just as Lucinda and I came downstairs to see what all the noise was about and she almost certainly and single-handedly saved your life.'

'How?' Nothing made sense.

Lucinda carried on the narrative. 'She stripped off your sleeve with a knife she kept and wound the ties of the curtains tightly around your upper arm and kept it raised. I think she pressed down on the wound as well and when the bleeding had slowed she took the blade to the fire and heated it before searing your flesh. All in the space of a few moments. When Dr MacLaren arrived, everything was over. All he did was to bandage the wound.'

'Is she here?'

'No. She left. Without a word to us. Grabbed the two knives on the floor and left.'

'I want her here.'

'She has gone from the Haversham town house.'

Taris walked forward and sat on the bed. 'I had the only servant the place boasted brought here and she intimated that Emma and Miriam were with other friends in London. She had no idea where.'

Asher tried to rise and fell backwards, the pain in his arm radiating around his whole body and making him feel dizzy.

'Doctor MacLaren said to warn you that if you move too much you will rupture the artery and bleed to death. He also said you were to have this.' Lucy emptied the contents of a sachet of powder into a glass of water and handed it to him.

'To stop it hurting,' she explained as he hesitated, and then smiled as he finished the lot.

'Stand guards around the house, Taris, and if you find Emma keep her here. Safe.' Asher felt the floating dizziness reach out and already the day was fading but he had to be certain his brother had heard. 'It is dangerous here. Everything is dangerous.'

He was pleased when Taris nodded, the tight anger on his face suggesting that the house would be watched over.

It was midnight when he woke again.

Emma sat in lad's clothes at the side of his bed, the tight line of her trousers emphasising the curves of her body. She held an assortment of sharp pins in her hand. Ungloved, he noticed. The searing red of the scars caught his attention, but tonight she did not seem to care.

'Stay still,' she whispered and placed a pin into his

skin below the elbow, twirling it this way and that. A small dull pain radiated up into his armpit.

'It will take away any infection,' she explained when she saw him looking. A dozen other such needles graced his arm and chest, catching the quiet dance of lamplight in their shivering thinness.

He tried to raise his hand to touch her, but he couldn't.

'Why…?' At least his voice still worked. She moved back, the frown on her brow deepening, but he was too tired to try to patch the story together tonight. All he wanted to know was Emma's part in it. He could not quite bring himself to say what he was thinking.

Why did you want me dead?

His eyes flickered uncertainly to the needles.

'They were island men,' she said quietly, anger resonating in every word.

'Are there more of them?'

'Yes.'

'They wanted to kill me.'

She was silent, though he could see the quick flash of temper that stormed through turquoise eyes. The unusual shade was muted tonight. Smoky. Distant.

'I will not let them.'

The absurdity of her vow almost made him laugh. He had no idea of how much time had passed since he had been hurt. One day? Two days? A week? Everything was blurred and difficult and when she bent down he tried to summon up his last reserve of energy.

'Look under the bed, Emma,' he instructed, pleased

when she did not question him, but leant down. 'Is that what they were after?'

A sharp spike of adrenalin raced through Emerald. Her father's ebony cane lay before her. Confused she laid it on the quilt. If Asher did not know of the secret compartment, she could slip the map out once he fell asleep. When she looked at him, however, she knew that the game was up.

'It was easy to open.'

'Open?' She tried to inject a great sense of surprise into the word.

'Move the catch and turn the body of wood to the right.' Said flatly as though he was running out of patience with the whole pretence. With trepidation she did as he instructed.

Nothing was inside save a sheet of paper twisted strangely to stop it from disappearing down into the sharp end of the cane. Removing it, she ironed it flat with the palm of her hand.

If you want what was in here you will need to trust me.

The ornate Carisbrook baronial seal was stamped on to the bottom in red wax and her shock was compounded by the wariness on Asher's face. It was all she could do to stop her voice from shaking.

'Where is the map?'

'I want a promise first.'

She stayed silent, not trusting her voice enough to speak. Where the hell would he have hidden it? Her eyes flashed around his room in a quick survey of possible places.

'Not here,' he continued. 'Falder is the only place I will return it to you and I want your promise to come there with me.

'I cannot—' He didn't let her finish.

'Where are your men?'

'Outside.'

'Bring them in.'

'Now?'

'Now.' The lighter webbing in his eyes was easily seen, giving him a dangerous and predatory look. Not willing to chance a denial, she walked across to the window and lifted a candle, waving it twice.

He noticed the sash had been raised. For her entrance, he supposed. And her exit. Lord, if he felt stronger this would have all been so much easier.

A man came through the window with a knife in his teeth and two pistols tucked into his belt and he was closely followed by a second.

Not servants at all, Asher thought, but pirates. He had had enough dealings with the likes of Beau Sandford to recognise those who scoured out a living on the open oceans. Lord, his ordered and controlled world was tipping up into more chaos by the second and he was angered anew by the silent questioning message that passed between the men and Emma.

Complicity and knowledge. They had seen the cane and it was impossible not to feel the flare of anticipation. Nothing quite made sense and the ache in his head blurred a nagging connection that he knew he should be making.

The burly Arab stationed himself at the door and Asher hoped that his sister would not take it on herself to grace him with one of her midnight visits. Taking a breath, he steeled himself to the task.

'I would like Lady Emma to stay here. With her aunt,' he added when he saw that she was about to argue.

'You what…?'

He ignored the smaller man's outburst completely and carried on in a measured tone. 'She will be chaperoned and protected.'

A slice of steel was the only answer. The knife at his throat pressed in before he could utter another word. He made himself relax.

'No, you will not hurt him.' Emma's voice shook and the knife melted away to be replaced by the angry dark visage of its owner.

'If you cross us, your Grace, the last thing you feel on this earth will be my blade.'

Asher laid back against the pillow. His head throbbed and the steady beat of blood in his ears made the world echo. Why did he not just give them the damn map and get them out of his life once and for all? Let them go back to Jamaica with the hard-won spoils of greed.

He knew the answer as he looked at Emma. Because, like it or not, they were connected somehow. He could almost feel the tie that bound them, and see in the turquoise depths of her eyes the same loneliness that was inside him. He'd felt it from the very first moment of seeing her at Jack's ball. Affinity. Alliance. Knowledge.

And the realisation that her prime motivation for being in England was greed had not bent him from his purpose.

A treasure map!

He noticed she had replaced her gloves before calling in her men. And yet she would show him the angry scars upon her hands. Nothing made sense.

'What did you want us here for?' The man at the door spoke for the first time. 'She could have told us what you have so far.'

'I want you to stand guard on the trip back to Falder. I will pay good clean gold for you to find the safest way back.'

The slur was not unheeded. 'And what do you get in return for all this?'

'The absolution of a debt.'

Emerald started at the words. Had he remembered her from the *Mariposa* or was it the incident after the Henshaw ball that he spoke of? Nothing showed in his face save exhaustion, the tinge of red around his irises giving him the look of someone who had ingested too much bad liquor.

Asher.

He had been as near death as she had seen anyone, the blood from the wound on his arm coursing across the floor in a red river, taking away consciousness and making him clammy. She put the image from her mind and walked to the window, raising her hand against the moon. Her fingers shook when she thought of it. Still.

Lord. The options closed in on her because she also knew enough about medicine to realise that for the next few days at least he should not be moved. And though his offer of a place here was appreciated, she could barely contemplate what his family must think of her.

The absolution of a debt.

The words floated in between the cracks of uneasiness and she felt both the power and the impossibility of them, for when she had torn off his shirt to tend to his wound she saw what she had not before.

Scars. Rows of them cut across his back, ribboned flesh silvered and sliced diagonally. She imagined the pain he must have felt and the sheer raw fury of powerlessness. She turned back to face the room, and when Azziz nodded she let out the breath she had not realised that she had been holding.

They would follow his instructions? They would take orders from a man who lay pale faced in a bed with a quarter of the blood that should have been flowing through his veins and the marks of slavery on his back?

Yes, they would, because, even given his wounds, leadership and authority stamped itself easily into the lines of Asher Wellingham's body and into the cadence of his words. A raw untamed wildness, all the more startling for the setting she had found it in. England. With its manners and protocols and ludicrous comportments.

For a moment she was disorientated with the sheer longing of reaching out and just holding on. He could protect her as he protected his brother and mother and sister. And the tenants on his land at Falder and the servants in all of his homes.

But she was Emerald Sandford and these dreams of safety were not for her. When she got the map, she would take ship for Jamaica, find the treasure and clear the debts that hung over her father's name. And then she would rebuild St Clair.

St Clair. Even the name was hard to say. She remembered crouching in the shadow of the trees with Ruby and watching the place burn, the flames lighting up the night sky for miles around, small pieces of ash floating into her sister's outstretched hand. Ruby had laughed as she had wept, waiting in the glade against the red, red sky; when the morning had finally come, leaving the skeleton of one remaining wall, they had picked through the rubble and salvaged three pots and a half-burned spade. And her jewellery box, slung beneath a beam that had not quite caught fire, a small buffer against impending poverty.

She shook her head and gestured to Azziz and Toro to wait outside. Using the moment of their departure to take the acupuncture needles from his arm, she found the darkness about his eyes worrying.

'A worthy art in the East, Emma, but here in England the pins may be misinterpreted for something else entirely.'

'What?'

'Witchcraft.'

She laughed at the absurdity of it, thinking of Wing-Jin and his patient teachings aboard the *Mariposa*.

'A society without rules is more dangerous then a

society with too many. Have you ever heard of the pirate Beau Sandford?'

The colour drained right out of her face. 'He was an acquaintance of my father's.'

'The devout and honourable Reverend?''

'The very religious treat each man as redeemable.'

She could barely utter the words said next. 'It is said that you killed this man?'

She expected him to brag about doing just that. But he didn't, and the pain in his eyes held her rooted to the spot, neither moving nor speaking.

My God, what had she done to him? His words from the night in the gardens at Falder came back to her. *'I was not at home for Melanie's funeral. I should have been home.'*

She had given his statement little notice before, imagining that perhaps he was on one of his ships plying the coast of foreign lands for cargo. Could there have been a more sinister reason for his absence and for his injuries and for the sleepless midnights when he wandered his library drink in hand and waited for the dawn? She turned to leave.

'No.' Asher's voice was tired, but he fought for consciousness with the same one-tracked determination as he seemed to fight everything else. 'You will stay, Emma. The deal. Promise me that you will.'

'I need to talk to Miriam.'

'No. It is not safe to leave.'

'My aunt will not understand what is happening.'

'Taris will speak with her.'

The lines between his nose and mouth were pronounced. He was exhausted, yet he still fought to have her stay. With him.

'This cannot be proper—' she began, but he broke across her words and smiled.

'Proper? When was anything proper between us?'

When she did not answer he rang the bell on his bedside table. Sweat beaded his upper lip.

'If you are in pain, I could help you.'

'No. Just…want your promise to stay.' His voice shook with exhaustion and his hair was dark and damp against the white of the sheets as he instructed his servant to see her to a room.

Chapter Ten

Emerald slipped through the kitchens into the garden. She had been at Carisbrook House for almost five days now, though she had not seen Asher since the day of her arrival. Her questions as to his state of health had all been answered perfunctorily by the servants, but had included no mention of an invite to see him and so she had stayed away.

Miriam had been installed in the room next to her and the cold her aunt was suffering seemed remarkably better with the ministrations of the Wellingham physician. This morning Emerald had sat reading to her, but now Emerald needed some space, some air and some exercise to temper the quiet edge of waiting.

The gardens, while not as large as those at Falder, were complex and the small sound of a boot scuffed against the shell path had her walking on further and turning a corner. Taris Wellingham sat on a wide marble garden seat, his hat in his lap and his face turned towards the sun.

'Lady Emma,' he said as he registered her presence.

'You knew it was me?' she said before realising the rudeness of such a question.

He smiled. 'Lack of sight heightens the hearing and you walk with a particular gait.' Tilting his head, he continued. 'You walk your world like one who is not at home in England.'

Emerald was still as she considered a response, though he did not seem to require one as he continued talking.

'If you sit with me for a moment, I would like to tell you a little about my brother.'

He waited as she rearranged her skirts and took a place beside him and when he started to talk she heard a reticence. 'Asher thinks that you need…protecting.'

'Does he?' She could barely answer.

'He thinks that you may be in trouble and he is a man who knows his responsibilities and sticks by them. Stability. Trust. Loyalty. All fine qualities, would you not agree?'

'I would.'

'And he is different since he met you, happier, for he has let few others close since his return from the Caribbean.'

Emerald frowned, uncertain now as to where this conversation was leading. Was it a warning?

'He was held captive for a year after the pirate Sandford ambushed his ship off Turks Island. And when a ransom note came to Falder and we finally found out where Asher was, he was full of only one thing—revenge. He came home only to get better to go back again a year later.'

Oh, God. Emerald tried to stop the aching lump of guilt that congealed in her throat from spilling over into her eyes.

This was all her fault.

When she had thrown Asher into the ocean as a means of saving him from the wrath of her father, no one could have foreseen the consequences. And this very minute was one of them.

She had ruined his life. Irrevocably. Undeniably.

'Emma?' His hand covered hers. 'Are you all right?'

'Yes.' She stood and forced a smile on her face.

Judas. Traitor. Liar.

If she saw Asher now, he would know.

Pleading a headache, she fled to her room and lay down on her blanket near the window, stuffing the fabric in her mouth to stop the sobs that gathered in the back of her throat.

All my fault...all my fault. The litany of guilt was like a mantra. His wife, his scars, Taris's lack of sight and his lost years. Lord, she had done all this to him. Unknowingly. The serpent in the Garden of Eden.

Her.

She crept down the corridor and across the stairs to the landing on the first floor.

Asher's rooms.

A spike of panic nearly had her turning away from the heavy door, but she made herself stand still until the fear had passed and then pressed on silently. Opening the door, she turned the key in the lock as she shut it behind her. It was dark inside and the glow from a fire in the grate of an adjoining room threw shadows over everything. A quick glance at the moon through the windows gave her a rough timing. Around three o'clock. She stood still until she had her bearings and listened until the scrape of a quill upon parchment drew her attention. He was writing at his desk? Her heart began to thud and the thin cotton shift she wore stuck to the moisture building across her skin. But she would not waver.

'Who's there?' His voice was close, husky, and she could not quite find it in herself to answer.

Emerald.

Beau's daughter.

Judas.

A chair scraped across parquet and then he was in the room, shirt-tails pulled from his trousers and wearing no cravat. Even in the lack of light she could make out the thick wedge of bandage beneath his shirt.

Was it too soon? Six days since the attack.

She placed her arms by her side and made herself relax.

'Emma?' A whisper of disbelief was underscored by soft puzzlement as his eyes came to rest upon her gloveless fingers. And, as if to give himself time, he asked a question.

'What happened?'

'They were burnt.'

'When you were cooking?'

Smiling at his assumption, she knew that she could not give Asher even one more lie. But there was something that she could give him. Something precious.

Herself.

Lifting her hands to the ties at her bodice, she unlaced the ribbon and simply stepped out of her shift, nipples puckering hard in the sudden cold.

'Lord.' Asher breathed in, and the sensual haze in his eyes took the breath from her body in one heavy hit.

'You once suggested a dalliance and I turned you down. I have come to think that was a mistake.'

She cursed the shiver that ran through her words and desperately wondered what was supposed to happen next. The growing thickness of his manhood was plainly seen, though she could not quite bring herself to lean down and open his laces. No, whilst she always swam in the nude and slept in the nude and was rarely hampered by society's penchant for undergarments, the pleasuring of a man was something she had only seen at a distance in the brothels of many a dockside port.

Wetting her lips with her tongue, she tried to remember the less bold moves of the doxies who haunted the drinking houses between Savannah la Mar and Kingston and with precision ran her hand across her stomach and lower, gently swaying her hips in the way Molly's girls did in the Golden Hind, a favourite drinking hole of her father's.

And now what?

A sudden fright consumed her. Would he be gentle? Worse, would he refuse her?

Asher saw the panic in her eyes before she closed them, turquoise bright and shaded by some emotion he could not quite fathom. What game did she play at? Would someone discover them and insist that he do the right thing by her and offer marriage? Marriage? To a woman who posed as a lady, acted the harlot and had the body of an angel. His eyes skimmed across her breasts. Her waist was tiny and the long length of her legs gave her a grace that was breathtaking. Lord, even at the salons of the select courtesans in London she would be exceptional, the tattoo on her breast and the scar on her thigh adding layers of mystery.

Lady Emma Seaton? Nothing about her quite added up but the sum total of all that she was drove him to the edge of reason.

He felt like locking her up at Falder where no other man would ever touch her again—she was his woman, damn it.

His woman?

The sheer possessiveness of the thought egged him on and he felt his rising lust as a power.

'Come.' He did not move at all, but waited as she walked forward into his arms, his erection hard against her stomach, pressing, eager, ready. When he shrugged out of his shirt, she touched the bandage gently, the pale gilt of her curls whisper soft against his cheek.

'Is it sore?'

Shaking his head, he removed his trousers and reached out to the curve of her waist and then lower.

Emerald felt the first push of his fingers in a place no man had touched before. Careful. Warm. Certain.

So this was it.

This was what she had heard of for ever.

'Asher?' She breathed his name as a quicksilver pain pierced her inside.

She would not stop him.

Payment.

Repayment.

Her repayment.

The guilt torn from her very soul made her still.

'Open for me, sweetheart.' The command was whispered and underlined by a quick movement. And when she did, the shards of gold in his eyes glowed against a darker brown. Triumph, conquest and elation mixed with desire.

The thick-cut pile of an Aubusson carpet beneath her back was warm as he laid her down and opened her thighs, his sex seeking an entrance, finding the pathway.

'I have not—'

He covered her mouth with his own and took away the words, his tongue mimicking the quiet thrust of his hips and her whole world exploded into pain. And then he was still. Desperately still.

'Lord. You're a virgin!' Rising above her, sweat beaded his brow and upper lip, the lines of his face softer now as tenderness stretched across desire. She tried to still him by holding her hands across his back, the firmness of muscle cut by ridged scars.

'Ahh, sweetheart. Why the hell didn't you tell me?'

The message was plain as his hooded glance sharpened, refocused, and she made to move out from underneath him.

'No, Emma. Give it a moment and the pain will pass.' He moved just slightly.

'It hurts.'

'I know. I know.'

He moved again. Forward this time. Deeper as he brought one arm beneath her back and tilted her hips. She felt the very hardness of him against her womb.

Kissing her gently, he nuzzled at her neck and ear. The cold trail of tongue across her nipple and fire consumed her. Without meaning to, she rocked forward. It was all he was waiting for, the pain less now as another feeling climbed. Higher. Closer.

'Come with me,' he murmured and, pulling her arms above her head with one hand, he turned her, the rhythm different, less known. A pause here. A deeper thrust there. His free hand held her bottom tight and he buried himself in her to the very hilt.

Up and up and up and over, the clenching waves of ecstasy made her jolt. Once, twice, more and more and more.

Spent, she lay lifeless and did not protest as Asher gathered her in his arms and laid her head upon his chest. Lying there in his shelter and listening to his heart while the wind gathered outside and chased clouds across the moon, she wished that time might just stop. Here. Now. For ever.

But the world ran on in the heavy chime of a clock and when his hand dropped she felt again the quick punch of sensuality.

'I still want you.' His words were quiet and the look in his eyes was sensuous, the scent of their lovemaking musky in the air. 'Do you want me? Again?'

When she nodded, he carefully rolled over and bent his elbows to her side to shelter her from his weight. The touch of his thumb against her breast was questioning; as her nipples hardened she pressed into his hand, her breath shallowed and waiting.

She was cold and he warmed her. She was hot and he cooled her. He was of her and she was of him and there seemed no place that they were separate or solitary in the heady secrets of the flesh.

And when he had finished he brought her up into his arms and walked across to his bed, gently laying her down and bringing up the sheets before joining her.

Smoothing back the damp curliness of her hair, he grinned. The golden lights in his eyes were easily seen and he looked younger and happier. 'We will be married as soon as the banns have been read. I swear it.'

Marriage!

God.

As who?

As Emerald Sandford?

She was pleased that he did not notice her confusion or her withdrawal as she lay there, listening to his breathing deepen into sleep.

How long would it be before Asher started to put the pieces together properly? Closing her eyes, she gritted her teeth. She could not tell him. He was an honourable man, a man who took his responsibilities seriously. And here she was, another responsibility, a woman whom he would feel bound to marry just because they had slept together.

Marriage.

In the circles she had mixed in, even the notion would seem ludicrous. But her father's crowd had never had the sort of moral fibre Asher Wellingham did.

A flare of pleasure warmed her and therein lay the rub, for her steely independence faltered somewhat under the mantle of his care, and if she let herself believe in fairy tales she would only be hurt all the worse later.

The memory of him deep inside her body made her heart race. Lord, but to never again know the sweetness of his kisses and the raw white heat of passion… She slashed at the tears that welled in her eyes and swore.

She was caught between love and lies, frozen into immobility. She, who had always walked her world unfettered and straight, the wind in her hair and the sun on her back and a sharp true blade in her fingers.

And now when her world had skewed and reshaped, she understood how often she had been lonely. Solitary. Isolated. Living in Jamaica under the shadow of her father had allowed no space for frivolity, for girlish pursuits, for love.

Love.

A prickling panic overcame her. Love? Asher had never said it. Not once. Could just lust be enough? Had it ever been enough for Beau?

She rubbed at the ache that was settling at her temples and promised herself honesty.

She was the pirate's daughter and already the whispers of her difference were starting, just as they had at home in Jamaica. She had never fitted anywhere. Even aboard the *Mariposa*.

Frowning, the slight echo of mistruth startled her. She did fit!

In Asher's arms with the promise of safety in his name and in the strong lines of his body.

Yes, for the first time in all her life she looked neither onwards nor backwards but existed just in the moment, a tiny and fragile reality that offered happiness.

Or hurt?

The ghost of her father hovered near and behind him other spectres lingered, death and pain written across each face.

She would not let them spoil this moment and she shook away memory, laying her arm alongside Asher and feeling his warmth. And then, when he did not stir, she pressed her legs against the long heat of his own and a shiver of delight consumed her.

When she woke again it was morning and the indent of where he had slumbered was still warm. He has only just left, she thought and sat up, running her fingers through her hair to try to straighten it. What should she do next? How many nights of loving constituted absolution? Rising from the rumpled bed, she was pleased to see that a basin with water and a towel had been left on the table. Wetting the flannel, she brought it across her forehead, her face in the mirror showing the struggle of wanting. Wanting to be with him. Wanting to be gone so that he might never know any of it. Today the blue in her eyes was overshadowed by dark, dark green and her hair was a wild array of wayward curls.

Not the face of a duchess.

She could not imagine a portrait of herself above the Carisbrook baronial fireplace to last down through the centuries. The scar that dissected her right eyebrow was reddened and visible and she brought up her finger to touch it. This was the sum of who she was and no amount of wishing it otherwise could preclude her past.

She had just dressed when he returned, and ridiculously she blushed. If he noticed, he gave no word of it—for that she was grateful.

'Would you walk with me? We have much to say to each other.' He did not touch her at all as she went past him and kept his distance still as they descended the stairs. Outside in the sun he seemed to relax more as they ambled between the stone walls, the lush green of summer in the leaves of trees that stood as sentinels on each side of the garden.

When he stopped she looked up at him. The brown of his irises was darker today and his hair slicked back as though he had just bathed.

'Who were the men who attacked me?'

So he wanted answers. She hoped that she might give him at least a version of the truth. 'The McIlverrays of Kingston Town. They want the map inside the cane. They believe that it should belong to them.'

'And you think it prudent to hold on to a treasure map that might indeed in the end kill you?'

She almost laughed at that, but stopped herself.

'My family has debts.'

His eyes narrowed. 'Tell me how much you owe and I'll place it into an account tomorrow.'

Her mouth fell open. 'No.' She couldn't do it, couldn't escape from here with a fat payment in her pocket after a quick toss in the sheets. That would make her—what? A whore? And every bit as on the game as the ones she had seen peddling their bodies in Jamaica. 'I can't take money from you like that.'

She was unprepared for his laughter. 'And what if you are pregnant?'

She had not even considered that.

'If you are pregnant, the child will be the heir to the Carisbrook fortune. I would not want him, or her, to be brought up on an empty quest for treasure or a hollow prophecy of greed. And Falder would welcome the promise of a child.'

'A child you would risk everything for?'

He shook his head and turned her towards him, peeling away restraint with a quick easiness. 'It is you I am trying to help.'

'Help me, then, by giving me the map.'

'And then watch you disappear?'

She reddened and felt his breath on the soft skin at the top of her ear and her insides twisted in longing. So simply done. So effortlessly won. A throbbing shot of warmth spread as she turned into his lips, groaning when his fingers flicked at her nipples. Even here, in the garden in the full view of the windows along the back end of Carisbrook House, she would let him have her, down on the ground amid the flowers and damn the consequences.

He was hers like no other person had ever been. She felt his familiarity with an ache, and was gasping as he drew back.

'This is not the place to... Come with me.' He led her to a summer house at the very bottom of the garden and stripped off his coat. The shirt he wore beneath was snowy white. After he loosened his breeches he stopped and smiled, the wind lifting his hair away from his throat and throwing a shadow into amber-lit eyes.

He was so beautiful. So masculinely perfect. With care she laid her palm against the rough stubble on his jaw and drew one finger across the fullness of his top lip.

'We could be seen—'

He stopped the words with a quick shake of his head.

'No. Not here.'

Suddenly she did not care. With a slow grace she undid the buttons at her throat, excited as he watched her lift the fullness of her breast above their protection of lawn and lace.

Wanton. Heedless. Immoderate.

She felt his fingers lifting her skirt and the wind on her shins and thighs and bottom as she accepted him with a sigh. Tipping her hips forward to get a deeper thrust his hands anchored her and she bit into the cotton of his sleeve to smother a scream.

'Easy, sweetheart,' he gentled, but she could not be still. The last trace of manners broke and she slid her fingers beneath his shirt and scraped her nails down the raised scars that marked his back. She was wild and free as he rubbed across the nub of hardness in the place where the swollen lips of her womanhood began, and when her head fell back the sunlight was bright upon her face.

She loved him.

'I love you.'

Had she said it? He stilled.

I love you. I love you. I love you.

Not yet, not now, not when he would not want it.

Not when the clenching joy of sex took her over the top of ecstasy and wrenched her on to the dizzy shores of elation.

Asher took her down with him as he collapsed on to the floor of the summer house. What the hell had just happened? He had emptied himself into Emma Seaton with an intensity he had never known possible and in the near-open, where anyone could find them. And with no thought to the consequences. He swore in amazement and kept her head against his shoulder, not wanting her at this moment to see his expression.

I love you. He had heard her say it and the words had melted the cold hard mantle of ice that had coated his heart since he had lost his wife. Since for ever.

Melanie. The soft whisk of an almost-breeze above him made him smile.

'I will have the banns read, Emma, and we can be married next month. At Falder in the chapel.'

When she looked up, tears magnified his face.

'There are things about me that you do not know. Would not like to know.'

'Tell me, then,' he answered and in his words she heard soft amusement. The amusement of a man who would imagine small digressions, little feminine faults. Tiny flaws and imperfections.

Lord, why was this not easier? She knew the answer as soon as she asked it. Because she had fallen in love with Asher Wellingham. And the promise of it was as sweet as it was forbidden. Not just the loss of her virginity now, but the sacrifice of her heart, and she was getting more and more caught up by the second.

Tell him the truth.

Tell him the truth.

A voice chanted in the back of her head, but she could not do it. Could not stand to see what was in his eyes now turn to hatred.

'Growing up in Jamaica was very different from here. The rules were very different. It was looser, less…moral?' She left a question at the end.

'Yet your father was strict?'

'In some things he was.'

*And in some other things, like the taking of life,
he wasn't.*

The image of herself as a ten-year-old, standing on
the deck of the *Mariposa* as her father slit the throat of
a slave, impinged over illusion. She had never had a
chance to become anything other than what she was
and for a moment she hated Beau with such a loathing
that she was shocked by it.

'After my mother went, there were things that I
should have learned…feminine things…that I did not
know…do not know still.'

He laughed and moved closer. 'I can see no glaring
faults in your upbringing, Emma, and I do not demand
a wife who excels in tapestry or singing or the mastery
of an instrument. Besides had you been raised here, you
almost certainly would not have swum naked from the
beach or gone to a bishop's house dressed in little more
than a gown. Or come to my room in your night shift
and offered me your virginity. I should be thanking
your father for the way that he brought you up.'

He leaned across to pluck a bud from the bush next
to him and tucked it in behind her right ear. 'In the
islands of the Pacific a woman promised to a man
wears a bloom here.'

Promised?

Her fingers came up to feel the soft wetness of the
petals and she made herself smile.

'You cannot possibly know what it is you are doing,
Emerald.' Miriam's voice quivered under the onslaught

of anger and the remains of her cough. 'Lord, child, but to bed him? To go ahead and actually fornicate with him... I cannot even contemplate what your parents would have thought of that.'

'I suspect my mother may have understood, given that she was sixteen when she was pregnant with me.' Emerald tried hard to hold on to what was left of her patience, though when her aunt went into another bout of a hacking cough she softened her voice. 'In Jamaica twenty-one would be considered old to be unaware of the pleasures of the flesh.'

'He must marry you, child. Surely he knows his duty as a gentleman...' Shock mixed with utter dismay.

'If I stood before the altar as Emma Seaton, I hardly think the marriage would be legal.'

'So you would have a child outside of wedlock?' Her aunt's old face was pinched.

'I am not certain if there even is a baby.'

'Pretend it, then. You are ruined already.'

'Pardon?' Emerald could not quite comprehend what her aunt meant, though the wily look in her eyes was familiar.

'The Carisbrook name is powerful. Pretend there is a child and marry him. As Emma Seaton if you need to. Who would know? You are young and fit. If a child did not come this month, then with the grace of God it will come in the next one.'

'I could not do that...'

'Oh, pah. Your father took away the future you should have had when he dragged you to sea for his

own gains, yet despite every handicap of birth and upbringing your heart is still in the right place. The Duke
of Carisbrook would be lucky to have you as a bride'

'Lucky? A marriage based on lies?'

'Untruth is often the result of need and circumstance; if life has taught you nothing else, it should
have at least taught you that.'

Emerald stared at her aunt, seeing clearly for the
first time the ghost of her dead father. The change
from the nervous and dithery old woman was amazing
as, for a second, Beau shone forth in the lines of her
face. Beguiling. Charming. Utterly selfish.

'It is wrong…'

'He is as lonely as you are and, if rumour is to be
believed, has been since the unfortunate and prema-
ture demise of his wife.'

'Which I caused.' Emerald had had enough. She
shouted the words, but as she dredged up the courage to
explain further Miriam began to laugh. Not softly either.

'Ahh, how the young torment themselves. You think
Melanie Wellingham would not have died anyway
from a bout of pneumonia after a cold long winter? You
think a storm could not have whipped her husband's
ship to the ends of this earth and blown him off course
to some other death?'

'No. I think that if he had not met my family, he might
be at Falder this very moment with a wife and children
and a brother who could see. And if I told him the truth
I could not bear to see the same thought in his eyes.'

'Because you love him?'

Emerald was silent.

I love you. She had said it to him once.

She was quieter as she answered and a thousand times more resolute. 'If I did as you bade me to, I would have to live all my life in a lie. Like my father did. Always careful, never honest with anyone, for ever looking over my shoulder for the past to catch up.'

Miriam sighed loudly as her hand came from beneath the bedcover. 'It can't have been easy on you, Emmie.' Cold fingers played with the band of lace on her gloves. 'I should have come out... insisted on some contact...for I knew my brother and he was not always such a biddable man to live with.'

Emerald shook her head. *Biddable?*

'I hate you. I hate you. I hate you.'

For a moment Emerald was transfixed by the rawness of her voice travelling through time from childhood, and was stunned by the sheer memory of animosity and ill will.

Biddable? She almost laughed at the understatement. No. There could be no happy ending. No small apologies or little mistakes. Lives had been lost and years had been taken; if the scars on her hands and her leg and her face had taught her anything, it was the fact that risk only brought regret. She shook her head and felt her resolve firming. Honesty was a policy that wreaked havoc on the good souls of those who had the misfortune to believe in it, and when she left England at least this way she would leave with her pride.

* * *

Asher came to her room after midnight, when the house was quiet. He looked tired and when he reached out she moved away.

A quota of penance? One night of loving for years of pain? It didn't quite seem fair somehow, but her withdrawal was fashioned from kindness. If he hated her, all this would be so much easier. For him.

'Last night was a mistake.' She couldn't even find it in her to be subtle.

'A mistake?'

'I am a lady and I was a virgin. You should not have bedded me.'

She thought she heard humour in his reply. 'Hard to determine experience with your robe pooled around your feet and the look of one well used to the art of lovemaking in your eyes.'

Reverting to character, she turned away and dabbed at her cheeks.

'I was an innocent…'

'To whom I offered marriage.'

'Because you felt guilty?' His silence confirmed all her fears and she was glad that he was not looking straight at her as she continued. 'I would rather not marry out of guilt, your Grace.'

'You think that is what my marriage proposal is?' There was an edge of irritation in his voice.

'Indeed I do. But do not worry yourself on my behalf—I shall be leaving for Jamaica soon to see to some property and I am not certain when it is I might return.'

'So you saved your virginity for some quick and meaningless affair? You expect me to believe that?'

When he came forward she meant to deny him, meant to hold up her head and plead the wrongness of it, but she couldn't. Instead her fingers fitted into his and she laid her head against his chest, feeling the careful touch of his thumb on her bare skin as it traced a line around the wings of her butterfly.

'Did it hurt?'

'No.' She smiled at the ridiculousness of the question in the whole face of what was between them.

'I want you, Emma. Now. Here. Tonight.' A breathless entreaty that set off an aching throb inside and took away denials.

'Just tonight, Asher. After this—' His finger rubbed across her lips and stopped the lies that were forming. And then she forgot everything that she had meant to say as the heat of his body seared into the answering warmth of her own.

She could barely look at him in the morning in the face of what they had shared until the dawn. Lord, even the thought of it drew a blush with the wetness of his seed on her thighs.

His seed. His lips against her and the promise of more in his eyes.

I love you.

She had said it again when her fingers had threaded

through his hair and the clenching throb of her sex had made her arch away from the unfamiliar softness of the mattress, and again when he had held her afterwards. Neither of them had slept even as the dawn broke against the windows and flooded the room with the light of day.

A perfect, balanced if-only love to remember when she was old and grey. The one moment to make every other subsequent second bearable.

When he left, she was glad that he went without giving her words that could bind them, badly, into a future.

Chapter Eleven

Asher parried with his sword, quickly, against the thrust of Jack's blade and brought the buttoned point to an unprotected throat.

'*Touché.*'

Even his voice sounded stronger and with the sun on his face and the image of Emma entwined around him he felt…unassailable, invulnerable, absolute, all feelings he had not known since…when? It was Emma Seaton's lack of need, her strength of purpose and an underlying will that bent to no one that made him like this.

'More practice, I think, Jack, if an ill man can beat you…'

'Hardly ill. You look better than I've seen you look in a long time.'

Asher turned away as guilt sliced into him. There were days now when he barely remembered the past, days when what had happened was blurrier, less real.

All that seemed true now was centred about Emma and her laughing turquoise eyes.

'I'm going back to Falder tomorrow.' He gestured to his arm, freed now from its bandage.

'Because you think they could try again?'

'If they do, I'll be ready this time—no one could surprise me there.' He slashed his blade through the air as if to underline intent.

'I'll see to my affairs and come up and join you before the end of the week.'

'I am not certain as to the safety of it.'

'You think it's that dangerous?'

'I do.'

'It's Emma Seaton, isn't it? All this has happened since she came. And now she's here under your wing? And her aunt, too, I've heard. Take care, Asher, for there are whispers.' A question lay in the air between them.

'Whispers?'

'Some say she is a fortune-hunter who targeted the largest fortune in London with her well-timed faint.'

'And what do you say, Jack?'

'I'd say, if she makes you happy who gives a damn about anyone else; besides, I like her too. She's different.'

After Jack had gone he stood in the gardens at the back of the house and lit a cheroot, pulling on it gratefully after the afternoon of exercise.

He had bedded Emma every night since shortly after the attack, and every night she had told him that she loved him.

My God. *Loved him.* If he had any guts he would have given her the words back. But he couldn't. Not yet. Not until he knew exactly who she was.

He screwed the sapphire ring on his finger around and around and made himself think.

She loved him, but she would not marry him. Why? When they arrived back at Falder, he would get the truth from her for London and the smaller house here hemmed them into properness.

Apart from the night time!

Grinding out the burning end of the cheroot beneath his feet, he wished he could go to her now and smiled as he looked at his timepiece. Four o'clock in the afternoon. For years he had dreaded the dark and now he welcomed it. Just another change she had fashioned in him. Another way she had made him different.

They lay on the covers, the fire in the grate sending flickering shadows across the walls and tingeing Asher's body with the soft glow of orange. His back was to her and her fingers traced the marks that stood up in knotted pearly welts.

She noticed how the skin on his forearm tightened at the contact and chanced a question.

'I saw marks like these once in Jamaica?'

She felt his interest.

'The man who sported them had seemingly lost his mind in a pirates' colony on Turks Island off the Silver Bank Passage. The law never took his ramblings seriously and so nothing was done, but I heard a few years later that the ship of an English lord had levelled the place clean away, blown it from the face of this earth with every last person standing in it, as revenge for what he had suffered there.'

'A fine tale,' he replied evenly.

'Your tale?' she questioned just as smoothly.

'I am a duke of the realm, Emma.'

'You are a man who keeps a blade hidden in the folds of his sleeve. I saw it at the Bishop's party and wondered why you should have a need of it here?'

'I had thought it well concealed.' His voice held the hint of respect. 'And besides…' His finger brushed over the puckered skin on her thigh. 'There are times when the childhood that you profess to does not quite add up. The mark of a sword and an indigo tattoo, flame-scarred hands and an excellence in the Chinese art of acupuncture. Truth be known, your secrets are probably every bit as heady as my own.'

She laughed to ease the tension, feeling his observations permeate the space between them. A hollow sort of sound that had his eyebrows rising.

'I said to you once before that I could protect you—'

Before he could finish she placed her finger across the smooth and full line of his lips.

'And I said to you once that there is nothing that you need to protect me from.'

He rolled on top of her so that she felt the hardening ridge of his manhood against the juncture of her legs.

'All my life I have been around women who have

needed…protecting. My mother, Lucy, Melanie. But you…you are different…stronger…'

Their eyes were at a level and the truth was suddenly important.

'I cannot marry you, Asher.'

'Why?'

'Because…because I cannot.'

'And yet you can be my mistress?'

She nodded before she could stop herself.

'Every night you tell me you love me. And sometimes when you sleep you speak in your dreams and you say it again.'

A single tear slipped from her eye and trailed its way down her cheek.

'If you would trust me.' He whispered it into the quiet of the night beneath the swathe of heavy curls under her right ear and she turned away, her fingers skimming across the dark red scar on his forearm. Still healing. A reminder of how fragile life really was and how easily it could be taken away.

If she lost him…

If she caused any of his family harm…

No, she would travel to Falder for the map and then she would be gone. It was the only honourable thing to do.

Chapter Twelve

The birdsong had only just started in the trees beside Carisbrook House when they left London. Robins, sparrows and finches, vying each other for the one perfect note. A quiet refrain, Emerald thought, compared with the ear-splitting cries of the birds back home in Jamaica.

Miriam, Lucy, Taris, Asher and herself sat in the second coach. In the first coach, full of the Wellingham servants, Toro sat on top with the driver. Emerald had seen the outline of the weapon concealed beneath his jacket as she had come down the steps to the street; she guessed that Azziz on their coach would be as well armed. It pleased her that Asher was taking the threat of the McIlverrays seriously and was allowing little chance of attack.

Feeling the warmth of him next to her, she looked across as he pulled the lush and ample furs over her knees. Today he was preoccupied, the brown in his eyes sharper than it usually was and blood from an ill-taken shave seen on his jawline.

'Are you warm enough?' He addressed the query to them all and refrained from catching her eye. She frowned. When he had come to her room last night, he had been slick with heat and want and need, but today the shadow of uncertainty lay between them, unspoken questions and impossible answers. Easier indeed to lose oneself in the promise of flesh, the darkness adding another layer of distance.

Lord, the whispered memories of night were like a shout in this confined space. Looking down, she saw the knuckles of his hand between them whitened to the bone. He felt it too, then? How could he not? She coughed to clear her throat and hoped that he did not hear the racing beat of her heart.

It was colder out of London, and the drizzle from yesterday had turned into a hard beating rain, the windows already fogged up from their breaths.

Emerald tried to see outside across the shoulders of her aunt and wished that she had made certain she was by the window. She had three knives concealed on her person and would have strapped her sword through her belt if she could have. But how? The shape of it could hardly be explained and this way her silent weapons held an element of surprise.

'You seem well recovered, Miriam.' Lucy leaned forward to speak more on the topic and Emerald used the moment to question Asher.

'How long do you expect us to take till Wickford?'

she asked. The town was the first stopover point, a place where the horses could be rested and watered and where there was a fair lunch served.

'Three to four hours in this weather,' he returned. 'More if the front to the west passes over us.' He rubbed at his arm as he spoke, giving her the impression that it was paining him. But she did not dare voice her concern with the others sitting so close.

'I noticed that Azziz and Toro were armed?'

He did look at her then. 'I can protect you, Emma. Do not worry.'

She almost laughed.

Worry.

My God.

She hoped he would not see the quick burst of temper. She had instructed Toro to make certain the inhabitants of the first carriage were safe before returning to help the second carriage should anything go amiss in their travels; although she could see that he did not care for the idea, she was sure that he would do as she had asked. Lord, this was all her fault and she prayed to God that they would need none of it and would journey to the Carisbrook property without mishap.

It was mid-afternoon when she noticed Asher turning in his seat to get a proper view of the land outside. Miriam was asleep, her gentle snores filling the silence of the coach. Taris dozed also and Lucy was reading a book. A romance about pirates, Emerald determined from the title and smiled at the cover.

Visions of the *Mariposa* came to mind, but she shook the memory back, into the folds of time. Here in England the image was unsettling. A few short weeks had given her a taste of what her life could have been like and for just a second she was overcome with the loss of it all.

Asher's hand slapping against the roof shocked her back to reality.

'Riders to the left,' he shouted, 'and they don't look friendly.' When he flipped open the catch of the window, light rain and wind slashed in, but he was already crouched across the seat, prying open the wooden box beneath the feet of his brother.

Three flintlock pistols lay nestled in a leather case and his fingers grasped the one nearest to him.

'Asher?' Taris's voice was flat and Lucy's book slid to the floor as she caught sight of the armoury.

'Get back against the seat. All of you.' He gave little notice to his family's fright as he opened up the door and lent out, his body arching against the force of wind and motion, the violent burst of gunfire loud even against the rushing noise of hooves and wheels and speed.

Lucy began to cry, and Miriam to cough and then the world as they knew it turned over, for the carriage, already hard-pressed in its escape, caught an edge and veered into nothingness, the screams of the women eerie in the slow-motioned silence.

Emerald came to on a bank not far from the carriage, the wheels still spinning against a muted sky.

She put her hand to her head to feel the hurt there. Bright blood stained her fingers and she winced as they explored a cut across her temple. Asher was some five hundred yards away from the carriage drawing the riders towards him. She heard him shouting something about the map and urging them to follow him before he disappeared into the undergrowth. Leading the McIlverrays away. From them.

Miriam and Lucy were huddled nearby and Azziz and Taris both out cold against a small embankment. Crawling across to them, she checked their pulses. Fast but steady.

Shots further off had her scrambling up and she grabbed her aunt's arm and entwined it around Lucy's.

'Run to the woods. Don't stop until you are far in and then dig down into the undergrowth and stay still.' When the girl didn't answer, Emerald shook her. 'I'll cover you from behind.' Lucy was sobbing in fright. Miriam said nothing, but the wide horrified stare of her eyes told another story.

Taking Azziz's blade, Emerald began to run, egging the two others on as she did so, the cool greenness of the forest dulling panic, and when a number of shots rang out across the glade she tried to pinpoint movement. Where was Asher now she thought? Where the hell had he gone?

Miriam seemed greatly recovered as she joined them and she instructed her aunt to take Lucinda further into the grove, though Asher's sister took hold of her arm as she finished speaking. 'No. You mustn't go. There is nothing any of us can do. Highwaymen are not to be—' She clapped her fingers to her mouth as a man broke cover not twenty yards from where they stood, the gun at his hip pointed at them, and murder in his eyes.

With absolutely no trace of hesitation Emerald whipped her knife from the soft folds of her boot and sent it rifling through space, the small thud as it connected with the newcomer's head almost ludicrous in proportion to the damage.

Two gawping faces confronted her as she turned, but she had no time for questions. Stripping the second knife from a hidden pocket, she cut the band of her heavy skirt and stepped from it. The thinner petticoat beneath would at least afford her a bit of freedom.

'Get into the forest. Miriam, make sure you don't come out unless you hear me calling. I'll cover your tracks.' Taking a branch from the nearest tree beneath the line of overhang so that it would not be seen, she pushed her aunt in the direction she wanted them to go before erasing the trail of their footsteps. It was all that she could do. Now she must find Asher and help him—if Toro had done as she asked and gone on, Asher would be alone in his battle with the McIlverrays.

'Lord help him,' she whispered under her breath as she circled back, the sum of years of tutelage having her automatically masking sound and her eyes keenly following the track that the single retainer had taken.

* * *

Asher felt the sharp sting of sweat obscure his vision and blinked to clear the blurriness. There were a number of men just behind him; as they came into a river valley, one gestured to the right. His heart sank. God knew how many he couldn't see, but, if he let them past, Emma and Taris and Lucy were less then a quarter of a mile back. And helpless. He'd checked Emma's pulse before he'd left her and his fingers had brushed across the gash at her temple. It was deep and his brother and Azziz were completely unconscious. His only help gone.

It was up to him.

Everybody was dependent on him.

Laying his pistol on the grass, he discarded his hat and filled it with damp leaves before jamming it through the sharp point of an oak sapling he'd cut. The shape and form of a head. It was just a little ruse, but it might work.

No. It *had* to work, he corrected himself as he jammed the stick into the earth and circled to the right. He still had time, for the group were talking to one another and laughing.

Easy prey.

He just had to take them off one by one until there was a manageable number. With four flints in his pocket and another two in the barrel he couldn't afford to waste ammunition on a miss. Fitting a polished river stone into his hand his eyes focused.

Closer. Closer. Steady. The stone arced across the

sky noiselessly and the chosen man fell hard. One down. He could not think about who else lurked in the deeper woods. The horses stopped and the more urgent sound of voices reached him on the wind. He could see that they scanned the valley for movement; turning, he lobbed another stone into the air to land in a rush of noise on the broad leaves of a sturdy bush.

It was enough. The hat from this distance gave an illusion of movement and the remaining men rushed forward. When he sighted them again, it was from slightly behind.

Perfect.

He brought the gun from his pocket and fired. Another man fell. And then another. Reloading, he sat to wait it out. Three more men left, though a scream of anger echoed through the trees, bringing with it the worrying sound of others.

More of the enemy materialised from the forest and he drew his sword, discarding the pistol in favour of blade as he backed up the embankment with careful steps and on to a ledge of thick brush. If they wanted to take him, he wouldn't make it easy. Here the horses could not follow and with him on foot the odds became more even.

Six men.

He had taken more.

Time slowed and focused. An easy balance and quiet waiting.

'Come on, come on,' he whispered and hoped he could kill a good number of them before they got to him.

* * *

Emerald saw him from above first, and even through her sheer terror and from this distance she recognised the style of his swordsmanship. My God, she thought as she scrambled down the incline, no wonder he killed my father, no wonder he cut a swathe through the men on the *Mariposa* like no others before him.

His was not an English style of fighting, but a foreign one. A style learnt not in the polite fencing salons of London, but in the world's godforsaken places, where fair play shattered in the face of sheer and brutal force.

She could barely look away. Already he had downed two men, but the others were circling closer and one held a gun.

They hadn't shot him! Hope blossomed. They wanted him alive as a pathway to the treasure. She shouted as a slice of steel creased the folds of the fabric on his jacket and red blood oozed through.

Asher heard the cry from one side and the flash of white petticoats had him turning.

Emma? With a sword in hand and a dirty bandana wrapped around the bright gilt of her curls? Memory turned, and against the dull grey sky he suddenly remembered what she must always have known.

'You!' He could barely believe it.

The girl from the *Mariposa*. Emma Seaton? He blinked twice just to make sure the image was real. And the turquoise eyes that looked back at him were dark in anguish.

A slash of steel to his right centered his focus and he waited to see whether she would raise her sword against him too. God. Could he kill her? For the first time in all his life he was afraid.

'You'll be wanting the map no doubt, Emerald.' The man nearest to him spoke, gesturing to those beside him to cease for the moment.

Emerald? Asher glanced sideways. Emerald? What sort of a name was that? Fragmented shards of memory clicked into place.

Emerald!

Emerald Sandford?

'The Duke has Beau's map hidden at Falder, Karl. If you kill him, you'll lose it.' Her voice was hard, distant, indifferent, as if the taking of his life was a meagre thing against the possession of what they both sought. In the pale light of a rapidly approaching dusk, the blood at her temple ran dark red, and the pallor of her skin made her look immeasurably older than the twenty-one years he knew her to have.

'You lie.' The older man opposite took up his sword and brought it down, fast. Quick reactions saved the blade from eating into her leg as she parried.

'If I had the map, do you think I'd still be here in England?'

With little effort she pushed his blade back and stood like one without a care in the world.

Like father, like daughter.

How easily they ruined lives. How little they thought of the consequence.

Pure untrammelled rage ripped through Asher.

Melanie. His brother. The aching remains of his right hand and the years they had stolen. Lunging forward, he scattered the circle, another man crumpling under the wicked sharpness of steel and all hell broke loose. In the moment of chaos he felt the small tickling whisper of a voice as Emma edged around behind him.

'Hate me later. I can help you now.'

With a well-timed quickness she plunged her blade through the closest renegade and turned to meet the next one and she fought as if a sword had been born in her hand. He frowned at the thought. Lord, it probably had been. The quick report of a gun close up made him stiffen, the smell of powder acrid in the air. In one movement he pulled his knife from his boot and hurled it before the man could reload, pleased when the blade easily found its target.

He kept her at his back, their paired position creating a circle of safety, the thrust and counter-thrust of the two men left easily beaten back. He heard the rasping of her breath and the quick noise of steel against steel. And then a lightly worded curse. She was tiring. He could see it in the way she held her blade. Parrying no longer, but defending. Why?

Gritting his teeth, he finished the fight. Quickly.

When silence again filtered through the clearing, Emerald found in her the strength to look up. And wished that she had not. Asher was furious and the clamp of his hand hurt the top of her arm. She swayed and would have fallen had he not steadied her. The sting in her side left her breathless and she didn't dare to look down to see the damage. Not yet. Not now.

He was sweating and in the last yellow light of the fading day the fury in his eyes glittered. 'You are the damn pirate's daughter? Beau Sandford's daughter? It was you on the ship…?'

'You have remembered?'

'Damned right I have.'

'I tried to make it up to you. Here and in London. In the bedroom. It was the only way I knew how.'

Even words were hard to say. Beneath the fabric of her jacket she felt the steady drip of blood. She looked down surreptitiously to make certain the white of her petticoat was not stained with red. If she could just be alone, she could remedy it. With the last surge of energy she pulled her arm away.

'My God.' Censure coated his curse. 'You saw our bedding as some sort of a sacrifice?'

'A payment. For my father. For me. We wronged you.'

'Wronged me? Lord, Emerald.' He rolled the name again around on his tongue. 'Emerald. Is that what I should call you now?'

'Some people call me Emmie.'

'But never Emma?' She shook her head as he waited.

'So everything was a lie?' The swollen flesh at the top of his lip creased into a humourless smile, and she refrained in the face of his anger to tell him the whole of it.

A lie?

To lie in the moonlight together and watch the way the light played off the hardened angle of his body. To feel his lips against her own, melding all that had once been into what now was.

Just a lie?

If he felt even a fiftieth of what she did for him, he could never have asked the question. Tears sprung to her eyes.

'Everything.'

One word and it was finished. She almost welcomed it when he turned away, for she could not see the hatred in his beautiful velvet eyes.

Laying her arm hard against her side, she followed him through the forest, pausing at this tree and that one to recatch her breath. He did not wait for her, did not look around to see her progress and for that small anger she was glad. Everything ached and the dizzy rush of blood in her ears was becoming louder. Lord, if the bullet had pierced her stomach... She shook her head, refusing to think about it, and was pleased when she saw Azziz standing against the upturned bulk of the carriage, his fingers rubbing the knot of a gash on the back of his head. Taris stood beside him, looking dazed.

'Where's Lucy and Miriam?' Asher's voice was hard as he looked around the clearing, and Emerald replied as Azziz stayed silent.

'In the woods. I told them to hide there.' She half-turned so that the right side of her body was hidden from him.

'Which way?'

'Over there.' It hurt to even lift her arm and point, the dragging red-hot pain worsened by movement. Let him go and find the others. Let him go soon before she was sick, before the whirling lightness overtook everything.

When he didn't move, she looked up.

'God.' he said roughly. 'My God,' he repeated and stormed towards her. 'What the hell has happened to you?'

His hand was warm against the cold of her own and she curled her fingers into his and held on. Anger she could deal with. Pity undid her. She felt the hot run of tears on her cheeks and hid her head against his jacket.

'Lord, Emma.' He used her old name, a small mistake as he pulled back her coat and his fingers were gentle against the wound, even as the roiling blackness claimed her and she fell into his arms.

Chapter Thirteen

Someone held her down. Hard. Hurting.

'Keep still, Emma!'

Emma! Emma?

Not her name. Nearly her name? Asher's face flew in and out of focus, the dark edges of a room behind, white candles burning on a desk.

Fragments. Memory. Her father mopping the blood from her brow and her mother in a corner. The same candles pushing back midnight.

'I need some more whisky…' The slurred voice of a drunk.

Her mother.

Evangeline.

Little angel.

Murderer.

In the blink of an eye she remembered everything that she had shut out as a six-year-old and, bringing the pillow across her ears, she began to shake. Hard liquor and the sound of screaming. The smell of whisky as a bottle broke. Shards of glass and the boozy face of Mother, close. Too close. Dangerous.

'Mama!' Her voice across the years. Young. Afraid. Unbelieving. She needed to get away. Out of the room. Into the dark of the trees around St Clair. Safety.

'Emerald.' Another voice. Softer. Huskier. Underlined with calm.

Asher was back. Against the shadows, his face impossibly handsome and the smell of drink receding against a different reality.

Falder. They were home.

'Home?' she whispered and watched as uncertainty kindled.

'Azziz and Taris?'

'Azziz is in the room next to this one, nursing three broken ribs and a sizeable lump on the back of his head. Taris escaped remarkably unhurt.'

'How long?' Full sentences were beyond her.

'You've been here for a week. But you have had the fever. It broke this morning.'

'Feel…strange.'

'It's the laudanum to take away pain from the wound in your side.' He stood up and stretched. The dark rings under his eyes were easily seen.

'Stay…please.' Suddenly she was afraid. Her mother crouched in the shadows with her madness and beyond that her father beckoned, tears streaming down his cheeks.

'James.' Curly-headed James. She had seen his

lifeless body buried in the fertile ground beneath the oak tree at St Clair before her father had calmly read the sermon and sent his wife away. Far from home. Far from them. Far from the grave of a son she had killed.

Emerald swallowed, trying to arrest the moisture that she could feel behind her eyes. Her childhood. The bones of secrets and lies. The product of falsity and hatred. Tears leaked out and fell down her cheeks, warm against a cooling skin.

She had lost them all. And now she was loosing Asher.

'I always loved you…since the *Mariposa*… I thought…I think…you are the most beautiful man I have ever seen.' She took the last of her pride and buried it. At least he would know. Her voice broke and she could not carry on.

Not just repayment, then.

When he said nothing, she turned over and shut him out. Shut them all out.

Just her.

She hated the way her chin wobbled as the strength that she always kept hold of broke into shattering sobs, but she could stop nothing.

It was over. Her life here was over and she could not even begin to imagine what she was going to do next.

The clock on the mantel marked the passing of silence as Asher watched her from above, her scar-traced hands linked across the pillow. Ruined hands like his own.

They had both been ruined by circumstance.

The thought knocked the breath from him. He had

spent five days listening to her rambling memories of childhood. Memories no one should have, memories fractured by madness and drink and death and dissolved into…what?

Blowing out the candles, he sat in the dark and when her breathing shallowed out he was glad. Looking down at the nightgown her aunt had carefully dressed her in, he noticed things he had not seen before.

The frail thinness of her bones and the way her hair curled beneath the fragile lobes of her ears.

God. Emerald Sandford. He should be furious. More than furious. His mind went back five years to the sea battle off the Turks Island Passage and he remembered other things. The soft feel of her lips against the nub of his thumb, the laughing turquoise eyes, the warmth of the day and the cold of the sea. He frowned. He had drawn back from the fight the moment he knew her to be a girl, and as he had dropped his guard she had retaliated with the hard edge of her sword and flipped him over the side.

Down into the cold of an angry sea where he had caught hold of the barrel she had thrown in after him, the roar of her father's anger loud on the air. Closing his eyes, he remembered other things. The circling sharks and a blood-red boiling sea. Thirty sailors on his ship and ten had survived.

Ten. He swore. Six by the time they had reached the coast and then only himself after a year in the pirates' compound.

Emerald Sandford.

Lord. His eyes ran across her full bottom lip and he laced his fingers together to stop himself from touching.

He wanted to shake her and he wanted to climb in beside her and hold her against the demons of her past. But he couldn't.

'*I love you.*' How many times had she said it? Would say it? The hollow shaft of memory held him bound by doubt.

As he let himself out of the room, he hated both her fragility and his intransigence.

She had lied, had continued to lie, her motivation based solely on the greed of treasure. Swearing, he walked down the hallway and out on to the balcony, relieved to feel the air on his face. Fresh. Clear. Cold. How long did it take for the sharp prick of vengeance to fade into a lesser ache? A quieter loss?

For ever, he decided, and felt a bone-deep shiver of guilt.

Emerald regained full consciousness just before the morning and lay very still, not wanting to waken the servant who sat dozing in a chair to one side of the bed.

Everything ached, but the mist that had consumed her was lessened.

They knew now. Knew who she was, knew who she had been. Asher. His mother. Taris. Lucinda. Her eyes fell to her hands. Gloveless. Exposed. Like she was. The scars red against the white of the sheet. She didn't even curl them up to hide them but turned her head to the window and watched the first pink blush of dawn on the high clouds outside.

Thus far she was safe. They had not taken her to Newgate. Or sent her to the poorhouse. No, she was still at Falder. In her room.

A portrait of Asher graced the far wall, his eyes watching with velvet gravity and their unexpected dance of gold. Behind him the house was caught in the last rays of a summer sun, the ocean sparkling to his left.

Falder.

As much as she might have liked to, she didn't belong here—she was a dangerous interloper from another world. A harsher world where the price of a life was measured in less than honour and where integrity and tradition were words other people used. *I love you.* She had said it again last night and wished that she hadn't even as the door opened and he walked in.

He had been riding. His clothes were splattered with dust and when he shut the door behind the departing servant she smiled. His manners were far better than her own. Another difference.

'I think we should talk.'

She nodded and looked directly at him. Beneath the façade of politeness she glimpsed a steely anger, held in check.

'You are Emerald Sandford, are you not?'

She nodded.

'Beau Sandford's daughter?'

Again she nodded.

'Who was it that taught you to fight?'

'My father. Azziz. Toro. Anyone with a bit of time to waste between watches on the *Mariposa*.'

'It was you on the boat, then? The girl who hit me?'

'Yes.'

'Why?'

'If you had stayed aboard, my father would have killed you. There were fifty men from the *Mariposa* and less than a dozen still fighting from the *Caroline*.' She stopped and looked away. 'He always killed those who were left and I thought, since you had given me a chance, that I should return the favour.'

'The favour?' Anger resonated around the room. 'The favour? Better to have lopped my head off then and there than the slow death you sentenced me to.'

'I did not know—'

He didn't let her finish.

'You are a pirate, Emerald.' The name came from his lips as if he did not even like the sound of it. 'You have killed people for your own gain.'

The horror in his words was palpable and, turning her head, she faced him, squarely. The past was the past and she could not change it. 'Believe what you will of me. I came here only for the map.' Her words were flat and she hated the sound of defeat in them, but she had no more to fight with.

'And that is all you want from me? Nothing else?'

Question quivered between them.

I want you to love me. I want you to take me in your arms and hold me safe. For ever.

She almost said it, but at the last second pinched the

underside of her left arm to stop herself. When she looked down the red crescent left by her nail on the skin was easily noticeable.

'The map,' she repeated with more conviction this time, 'is all that I want from you.'

He nodded and stood, hands in the pocket of his coat and feet apart, as a sailor might have stood on the deck in a storm. Distant. Lonely. Distracted. 'I have instructed everyone here to keep the secret of your identity. For the moment you are safe. But when you feel better, I would rather that you did not venture outside this room without somebody at your side.'

'Because you feel I might be a risk to your family?' A hollow ache pierced her as he looked up and the blank indifference in his eyes broke her heart.

'I will provide passage to Jamaica for you when you want it. On my ship out of Thornfield.'

She could only nod this time, the thick sadness in her throat rendering speech difficult.

'And if you should need money—'

She stopped him. 'No. Just the map.'

As he turned for the door, the dizzy whorl of relief hit her. Another moment and she would have caught at his hand and begged him for even the scraps of love.

Like. Friendship. Esteem.

Even they might have been enough.

Outside Asher laid his head back against the oak door and took in his breath. Lord, Beau Sandford's daughter. What the hell was he to do with her? She had countered the McIlverray threat with a bravery that had stunned him and had slept with him as a repayment for the hurt done to his family. His teeth ground together as he thought of the hurt he had done to her family.

An equal revenge?

For the first time in days, anger loosened its hold. Perhaps all was not lost. Perhaps in the last threshold of truth something could be salvaged. He imagined Emma…no, Emerald, in satin and silk dancing, candlelight in her hair and the hint of laughter on her lips.

Laughter.

When had she had that in her life? When had she had frivolity or joy or easiness? Not with her mother or Beau. Not since coming to England either, that much was sure.

His eyes flickered to his right hand and he flexed it. Today he felt no movement or sensation in his ghost fingers, another passing reminder of change. Five years since the *Mariposa* had overcome his ship. He did a quick calculation. She must have been, *what*…all of sixteen, perhaps? Younger than Lucinda and expected to fight a man? More than one man? The scars on her hand and face and thigh told him that.

By God, if Sandford was here right now he would kill him again just for the hurt he had done his daughter—she had never stood a chance against the greedy underbelly of that world.

And yet somewhere in the darkness of her upbringing she had discovered and fostered integrity and responsibility. Servants and an aunt she would not abandon and a handful of others to whom she felt allegiance. And when she had seen him at risk she had jumped in to the rescue without a thought for her own well-being.

If it was only the map she truly wanted, why would she do that? Better to let McIlverray do his worst and head by herself for Falder and the map.

I love you.

Perhaps she had truly meant it. Not just atonement, but something deeper. More lasting. True. He flattened his fingers out against the wall at his back and tried to take stock of the whole situation, tried to stop the heavy throb in his loins from clouding reason.

Emerald sat up in bed and ate the lunch that had been provided for her. She had not seen Asher since yesterday and Miriam had heard that he was in London on business. She hoped he was safe.

Lucinda and Alice had both visited her that morning and both had looked at her with something akin to wariness.

'You did not tell us of your skill with a knife and sword, Emmie—' Lucinda stopped. She said the name with uncertainty, as if just the mention of it might conjure up the steamy Caribbean underworld. 'Why, when you sent that knife across the clearing and hit that man I could barely believe it—' Again she stopped and her mouth fell into an even greater gape. 'It was you wasn't it, on the dockside with the Earl of Westleigh. It was you, who saved me? You're Liam

Kingston?' She blushed profusely. 'I should have known it was you. The gloves. Your height. Lord, it was you all along.'

Emerald could do nothing more than nod, though, as she chanced a look at Asher's mother, she was surprised by the gratitude that shone from her eyes.

'You have saved us all from harm, my dear, and I do not know how it is we will ever be able to thank you.'

The thought did cross her mind that such generosity was misplaced, given she had brought the McIlverrays to England in the first place, but she took Alice's offered hand and held it tightly, and the older woman did not pull away or look askance at the scars that blemished the skin beneath her knuckles.

They had seen exactly who it was she was and still they thanked her. For this moment she felt humbled by the generosity of a family who had much reason to hate her. Unbidden tears welled in her eyes. How she wanted Alice and Lucinda and Taris to like her.

Asher's family.

At least then, when she was gone, they would remember her fondly. She dabbed at her eyes and was horrified when still more tears welled. She never cried. Never.

Turning her head into the pillow, she was glad when she heard them leave.

When the last rays of orange were fading from the far-off hills, there was a knock on the door.

This time it was Taris who came into the room.

Carefully. She could tell that he was not often here, given the number of times he bumped into things. The table in the middle of the room and the chair near the fireplace. He always stood against the light of the window, she thought, as he stopped there.

'Asher tells me that you blame yourself for this.' His fingers swept up across his eyes and he was still. Waiting. Emerald took a breath. It was rare in England to find people who came straight to the point and she liked him for it.

'If Asher had not met my father—'

He stopped her. 'You do not strike me as a woman who qualifies her life much with "if". If I had not done this…if only I had done that…'

Despite everything she smiled. What was it Taris had said of blindness? Other senses were heightened? Certainly he seemed to have the measure of her and it was easy to be comfortable with him.

'My father was a man who felt that the oceans were his own. Any oceans, but more especially those around the Turks Island Passage. If he had not seen the *Caroline* that day—' She stopped as she saw his lips twitch and rephrased her words. 'Your loss of sight was a direct result of my father's greed.'

'My loss of sight was a direct result of my own need to protect my brother; if it had not happened in the Caribbean, it might have happened somewhere else. On the high mast of an ocean-bound ship or in the slow roll of a carriage on the hills before Falder. Fate, Emerald, or destiny. Call it what you will. I do not blame him and I do not blame you. There is, however, something that you could do for me.'

'Yes?'

'Marry Asher.'

She almost laughed, but stopped herself at the last moment. He was deadly serious. She could see it in every line of his face.

'I think marriage is the last thing that your brother would want from me.'

'You are the only one who can save him.'

'Save him from what?'

'From himself. He blames himself for everything.' He reached down to feel the seat of the chair beside him and lowered himself into it before continuing. 'When Melanie caught a cold, she went to bed with camphor and honey drinks. When it got worse, the doctor was called. And when it got worse still, my mother held her hand while she breathed her last. If Asher had been at Falder, the result would have been exactly the same. He could not have saved her. But a healthy person can die inside just as easily as a sick one and that is what he has done. Ever since.'

Emerald was astonished. She could barely believe what he was saying to her. The power of it! And Taris was close to his brother. Close enough to truly know what drove him, what hurt him, what made him who he was. Could what he said be true? Could she help him in the same way that he had helped her?

'Don't give up on him. Not yet. Can you at least promise me that?'

She took in a breath and nodded because she didn't trust herself enough to speak and then she smiled. He would not see the movement.

'Thank you.'

'You saw me nod?'

'I felt it. In the shift of light.'

'Where is Asher?' she added as he stood to leave.

'He went to London on business. We have a number of ships due out to India.'

Emerald heard frustration in his voice. 'In Jamaica I had dealings with a witch doctor who could heal just about anything—even some loss of sight.'

He laughed, a rich deep sound that resonated around the room. 'You are the very first person to mention my affliction in the same breath as divulging a cure, Emerald. Yes indeed, you should suit our family well.'

And with that he was gone.

Asher spent the next week trying to make sense of everything that had happened, trying to dull the effect that Emerald Sandford had made on him and trying to get his life back into some sort of order.

On the third day in London he found himself in an establishment off Curzon Street; the moment he walked through the front doors, he knew it was a mistake.

Angela Cartwright, a handsome red-haired woman met him as he removed his gloves and hat, the neckline of her gown perilously low. Last time he had been here he had admired her obvious endowments. This time all he could think about were smaller breasts topped with shell-pink nipples and a liberal smattering of freckles.

Emerald.

To be thinking of her in a place like this worried him and he resolved to put her from his mind.

'Why, your Grace, it has been some time since we have seen you here. All of six months, would it not be, Brigitte?'

A beautiful girl, standing against the far wall of the parlour, came forward, her light blue eyes alive with laughter and her brown hair caught in an intricate style at the back of her head before the length of silk tresses fell to her waist.

'Indeed, your Grace. I think you were here last time with your friend Lord Henshaw. Is he well?'

'Very.' Accepting brandy, Asher drank heavily, reasoning that tonight he needed all the fortification he could get.

'Perhaps I could show you the conservatory, your Grace,' she added as she renewed his drink from a crystal decanter. 'It is the latest addition to our household and has been very well received.'

On the edges of her practised French accent lingered the twang of the Covent Garden markets. Normally the contradictions would have amused him, but tonight he was vaguely angered by it, and bothered too by the over-embellished furniture and paintings depicting cherubs in various stages of undress. This place was the most exclusive of all the London brothels, yet it felt cheap in a way that it hadn't before. And the churning dread in his stomach had absolutely nothing to do with anticipation.

In the conservatory, any inhibitions that Brigitte had displayed seemed largely gone and when he felt her fingers suggestively cup his genitals he moved back sharply.

Lord, why was he here?

Why was he not home at Falder with the green hills all about him and the beating ocean in the distance? And Emerald Sandford in his bed, warm and willing and beautiful? Because she was a liar and a cheat and the daughter of Beau Sandford and because everything she had ever told him had been based on her skewed version of the truth.

A room to one end of the structure had been fashioned into a bedchamber, its large four-poster draped in lawn. When Brigitte raised her arms to loosen her hairpins, he marvelled that the sight did not affect him in the least. All he wanted was gold mixed with red and entwined with the lightest of corn.

Emerald.

He made himself come forward and draw a finger against the warm smoothness of Brigitte's skin, trailing his touch along the base of her jaw and down again into the softer places. A swelling bosom and milk-white complexion, the fat abundance of womanhood warm and pliable in his hands as she tipped back her head and groaned.

Emerald. He wanted Emerald. He wanted her joy and her fierce independence. He wanted the feel of her against him as they lay under the full light of a new moon, his ruined fingers curled into hers. Disorientated, he stood back and looked around. Uncertain. Desperate. To leave.

'I am sorry,' he said quietly, jamming a coin into her hand before moving away.

Away from the wrongness of Curzon Street, its inherent loneliness tempered only by rich fine drink and impossible dreams. This was not the way to forget Emerald. This was not the way to claw back a future and find again in his life a place where sheer emptiness did not consume him.

When he was outside he laid his head against the side of the building and thought.

The port beckoned as it always had with its freedom and smell and foreverness. The infinite blue of the waves and a horizon that did not finish. Adventure, new lands, the riches of the colonies spilling into his holds, spices, silks, tea.

As his driver pulled into the curb near him, he walked briskly across and ordered the coach to the docks. His newest sloop was a few weeks away from completion and he would benefit from a good bout of hard work.

Chapter Fourteen

She found the map on her bed after returning from a walk around the kitchen gardens with Alice.

Asher. He was back. He must have waited until he knew her to be gone from this chamber before depositing the parchment. It had been eight days since she had seen him and the exhaustion that had kept her in bed had dissipated into intermittent tiredness, and then disappeared altogether as the wounds at her waist healed into an itchy red.

Unrolling the parchment, her eyes skimmed across the tangents indicated. True west of Powell Point on the tip of the Ship Chan Cay. And a date. 1808. The year after her mother had gone. The year her father had acquired the *Mariposa* and dispensed with his life as a lord.

Tucking the paper into the middle of a book to make certain that the edges were unseen, a new and more worrying thought struck her. Was this Asher Wellingham's final goodbye gesture? Had he not said he would give her the map and provide transport home?

A knock at the door made her jump. The footman outside bowed his head as she caught his eye.

'His Grace requests your company, my lady. He asked me to bring you to him directly.'

Resisting the temptation to go to the mirror and tidy her hair, she pulled at the material in her skirt so that it fell to a more decent length, a slice of pain worrying her side at the movement. Only a scar where the bullet had been extracted, the doctor hurried from London both skilful and competent.

She had been lucky in more ways than one; the McIlverrays were all dead and no longer a threat and the local constabulary was treating the whole incident as highway robbery. Asher with his wide connections had made certain that no trace of scandal ensued. Nothing to touch her. Nothing to hide from.

She smiled as she saw him standing against the open French doors. The gardens behind framed the blackness of his hair, and his clothes were casual, breeches tucked into brown boots and his white shirt open. Her heartbeat began to race as she pushed down the familiar, aching, breathless want for him.

Don't touch him.

Don't let him near.

Don't let him see how much he has hurt me, could still hurt me.

'Good morning, Emerald. You look well.' He made no move to take her hand or come closer. There were no hooded glances or any suggestion of a shared intimacy. Rather he held back, unstintingly correct as he acknowledged her presence.

Today his eyes were the darkest that she had seen them, not even a shimmer of gold visible.

'Thank you for the map.' It was all that she could think of to say. After everything.

Wariness crept into his face. 'You will return to Jamaica to search for its bounty?'

'Yes. It should be easy to read the co-ordinates.'

'How?'

'How?'

'How will you do that?' His question was inflected with a controlled impatience and she was silent. What ship could she use? No one would give her credit in Jamaica and, with the loss of St Clair, she had neither property nor chattels to bargain with. A further lump blocked her throat. He would be rid of her this easily?

'I am not certain.' She made her voice even, indifferent, as though the matter of a vessel in which to travel was but a small and trifling consideration.

'As I said, the *Nautilus* is due for a sea run.'

She could not quite understand what it was he was telling her.

'If you needed passage, I could provide it.' His voice held an iron edge of control as he spoke again.

'Why?'

'Because you were a virgin.' So easily said. So dismissive of emotion.

She marched over until they were face to face. 'I am

not pregnant.' The sheer stupidity of her remark made her blush, but his detachment was more hurtful than anything else and she didn't want him to think that he was bound to her by non-existent ties.

'My offer is not conditional on the production of an heir.' She felt the whisper of his breath on her cheek before he moved back, and wanted to reach out and touch the warmth.

This whole conversation was so absurd she suddenly felt tired by it all. The hope. The lack of hope. The see-saw of emotion. The second-guessing as to how he felt. Love me? Love me not? Like the old game she had played as a child with the few other children who were allowed in her company. All she wanted to do was to step forward into his arms and feel their strength around her. Keeping her safe. From everything.

The low wheeling of a gull pulled her attention skywards. Today the weather was fresh, though a bank of clouds sat heavy in the west. There would be rain again later. She was certain of it. Unmindful, she drew her hand across the ache in her side.

'It hurts?'

'Sometimes. Less now than before.'

'I didn't see it happen.'

'It was the pistol. One of the McIlverrays saw my lack of attention and took his chance.'

'You hold your sword like a man does.'

'I was taught by men.'

'And Ruby? Who is Ruby? You spoke of her in your fever dreams.'

'My sister. Beau's daughter by one of the dock-side harlots. Her mother abandoned her before her second birthday.'

'Where is she now?'

'In a convent in Jamaica.' Even the saying of it made worry surface. How would her sister be coping in the care of the nuns, for though they were eminently understanding and kind, they were still strangers. 'She is eight and loves music. I taught her to play the harmonica and she tended the gardens at St Clair with some help from me.'

'St Clair is your family house?'

'Was. It was destroyed last summer by the McIlverrays in their search for my father's map.'

'Where have you lived since?'

'On the docks in a room off the Harbour Road until Miriam sent us money for a passage to London.'

'And if the treasure that you seek cannot be found, what then?'

She didn't answer. Couldn't answer. Reaching for the locket around her neck, she rubbed the gold in a way she had done in all the other difficult moments of her life. A small ritual. A way to be closer to—what? The bauble had come from a time in England when the family had been happy and whole. A time before drink had ripped the heart out of everything.

'I saw Annabelle Graveson in Thornfield and she was asking after your health. She gave me this.' He brought a book from the satchel at his feet and handed it to her.

The burgundy leather that bound the cover was so

old it had split across the spine; as she opened the cover, there was a name. Evangeline Montrose. A woodcut of the same design as that of her necklace was etched below it.

One finger reached out to trace the letters as she struggled with the connection.

'My mother's name was Evangeline,' she said finally, feeling the turn of something forbidden shift, and crystallise as Asher spoke.

'And Annabelle's maiden name was Montrose. She said your mother was her cousin.'

Annabelle Montrose. Evangeline Montrose. Cousins. The crest of their family emblazoned on book and locket. The same.

She could barely take the whole idea in. 'You knew?'

'I remembered the locket when I was at Annabelle's last week and saw the design carved upon her crest. Today Annabelle seemed more than upset when she handed the book over.'

'Do you think she is stable?' Emerald asked the question even as she meant not to.

'Stable?' He tilted his head slightly as though trying to catch her meaning.

'In her head. My mother wasn't, you see.' A cold chill of dread seeped into Emerald's blood. Madness? Was it not a family trait? The air around her felt suddenly heavy, the sun that had been out a moment ago lost behind heavy cloud.

June.

Where would she be by July?

And why would the socially conscious Annabelle Graveson risk the exposure of such a damning family skeleton? It didn't make sense. Another darker thought surfaced. Did Annabelle mean to use this as a warning?

After all, she had not given the book directly to her, and Jack Henshaw had said that Asher was the trustee of the Gravesons' affairs. Was it him she was trying to protect?

All this introspection made her head ache. If Asher had looked at her with even a glimmer of want in his eyes, everything would have been so much easier. If he had taken her hand in his own even lightly, she might have clung on and risked it all. But he barely glanced at her, the tapping of his fingers against the side of his thigh giving her the singular impression that he was impatient for her to be gone.

'The *Nautilus* will sail in four days' time, so, if you would like to speak with Annabelle it would need to be arranged soon. I think you could count on her silence as any scandal could by association also affect her reputation and I doubt that she would risk it.'

She nodded, her person relegated now to merely scandal and risk. Someone to be shoved on a boat and sent home before she could do any more damage. Like the remittance men she sometimes saw wandering around the gambling halls of Kingston Town.

For ever outcast.

And conveniently forgotten. Even the thought twisted as pain inside her.

To never see Asher again, to never feel him beside

her in the night when the ghosts of memory were strong and only he could quell them. To never walk the green hills of Falder or be a part of a family that had taken her in without question. Unequivocally.

Her chin lifted. She would not grovel—she had Ruby to think of and Miriam. If she could recover even some of the treasure, they would be safer.

'Could I have the use of your ship for a week in Jamaica?"

'To plot the co-ordinates from the map?'

'Yes.' She looked at him directly. One promise and she would be gone.

When he nodded she let go of the breath she had not realised she was holding. 'Peter Drummond is to be trusted, if you should be lucky enough to find anything.'

You. Not us. He did not mean to come with her then? 'Thank you.' She felt her teeth sink into the soft flesh on the inside of her mouth as she bit down to stop herself from saying more and watched as he bent to collect his satchel.

'I shall send a note to Annabelle Graveson within the hour and will let you know of her reply as soon I have it.'

When he walked away, birdsong muffled his footsteps, and she was left to find her own way back to the suite she shared with Miriam.

Her aunt was working on a tapestry and sitting near the window in a sitting room that came directly off her bedchamber.

'Was my mother's name Evangeline Montrose?' The answering shock was plain in her aunt's eyes. 'Annabelle Graveson gave Asher this book.' Opening the cover, she held it on top of Miriam's sewing, digging into the bodice of her gown and extracting the silver locket. 'Her maiden name was also Montrose. They were cousins.'

Miriam placed the sewing on the table beside her, her face white with shock. 'I did not know that. Can she be trusted?' Her voice was strained.

'Not to spread our secret?' She waited until her aunt nodded. 'I should imagine she wants her association with my father known to as few people as possible. For us…I am not sure how much anything matters. We are leaving England on one of the Wellingham ships bound for Jamaica in four days.'

'And Asher Wellingham…'

'Will be pleased to see the back of us I think.'

'I am sorry, Emmie…' But Emerald held out her hand and stopped the sentiment, swallowing back the lump that had formed in her throat before striding through to her own room and shutting the door.

Once inside, she brought her fingers across her mouth and breathed into them heavily, a silent scream of frustration, anger and grief. Grief for the loss of all that was gone. Picking up the book, she traced her finger across the name at the top of the inside cover and held it close to her chest.

When had her mother written this? Where had she written this? Before she had met Beau? After she had gone out to Jamaica?

She had no pictures at all of Evangeline, only the vague recollection of a voice. Standing, she walked to the mirror and looked at her own reflection. Some of her father stared back at her. She had his eyes and chin. She had his height and colour of skin. But her dimples? Where had they come from? And her hair? Beau's hair had been dark and straight, and thin in his last years. Differences.

Chapter Fifteen

Asher left Falder and visited his jeweller in the centre of London the next morning, even the thought of the gossip that would be rife as a result not swaying his purpose.

He had always lived in the glare of the public eye, his time away giving the tattle-tongues much to conjecture upon; on his return to England as a widower there had been relentless speculation. Speculation that he had used to his advantage—sometimes in the salons of London he could almost feel the sharp taste of fear as others carefully tiptoed around his lost years and his scars.

And his retribution.

Beau Sandford.

It was said that he had run the pirate through the stomach a hundred times just to make sure that he was dead and then sliced off his ears and hands to feed them to the circling sharks below. And laughed as he had done it.

Jack had told him that once after a particularly harrowing dinner party when he was newly returned home, and since then he had restricted his socialising to the houses of friends.

Killing took a part of your soul, no matter how warranted the deed. After he had run Beau Sandford through the heart and watched him drop into the ocean below, he had turned away and fought down bile. And the anger that had consumed him was replaced instead by a kind of shame. Shame for where his life had taken him. Shame because as the Duke of Carisbrook he should have been able to protect his wife and his brother, kept them safe. Kept the English sense of honour and goodness intact. Even the Carisbrook crest reflected that.

An elk with its pointed horns and the rose of England between them, 'Onwards and upwards' printed at its base. Such an English sentiment. Eminently honourable and unwaveringly good. The sum of generations of dukes, their stewardship of the land marred only occasionally by some far-off crisis.

Except for him.

And yet even for him Falder closed around him with its green valleys and woods, with its clear streams and the never-endingness of sea, with its mirrored turrets and carved stone gates.

Falder.

Home.

For the first time he saw that in tradition there was safety and healing and regeneration. The beginnings of another reality. For them all.

For Emerald and Taris and for the ghost of Melanie. And for himself. He smiled and breathed in deeply as Peter Solbourne, his jeweller, met him at the door.

'I was about to send you a message, your Grace. You had mentioned your desire to find a gift for your sister's forthcoming birthday the last time you came to see me and I thought that these just may suit.' He brought forth a burgundy box strangely carved.

E. S. 1801.

The design was interwoven with lines of silver and these in turn were embellished with stones. As the jeweller undid a catch to one side of the box and lifted the lid, Ashe caught his breath. Pearls. Rose-blushed and graded from large to small, the lustre on them attesting to the purity of the shell.

'My God.' He lifted the necklace from its bed of silk and placed a finger against the last roundel. 'Where did you get these?'

'A man brought them in two weeks ago. A most unusual fellow. I have had them certified. They're from the islands around the Caribbean.'

The hair on the back of Asher's neck bristled. 'Did he give a name?'

'No, your Grace, he did not. Oh, he did leave a card for future reference. The Countess of Haversham's card, actually. I thought it most odd at the time. But he made me promise to let her know who had bought them.'

Asher instantly ceased his questioning. Lord! E. S. *Emma Seaton! Emerald Sandford!* Could these be her pearls? He held them closer.

'How much are they?'

When the jeweller gave him the price, he doubted she would have received even a tenth of the exorbitant amount mentioned.

'I'll take them.'

Solborne looked astonished at the ease of the deal and promptly returned the strand to its bed before handing over the box. 'Is there anything else, your Grace?'

The gleam of interest in the old jeweller's eyes was easily seen. 'I would like to see a selection of your very finest rings. Emeralds. The stone must be an emerald.' He was pleased when Solborne did not query him further.

Twenty minutes later he had made his choice, a narrow gold ring with a large peerless emerald edged in smaller diamonds.

'A fine choice, if I might say so, your Grace, and I am certain that the lady for whom this is destined will be more than pleased.'

'And there is one more thing that you could do for me,' he added just as he was about to leave. 'I want you to make no mention of my purchases. It's a surprise, you see, and I should not want word to get around.'

'Indeed, your Grace. My lips shall be sealed.'

'Good.' Tucking the two boxes into his jacket pocket, he showed himself out and instructed his driver to take him to Madame Berenger's dress shop. He hoped the seamstress would have a selection of ready-made gowns to choose from, for he did not have the time to wait.

Chapter Sixteen

Annabelle Graveson brought a large case of family letters and sketches of Evangeline when she came to Falder and the rather stiff woman who had given them dinner at Longacres all those weeks ago was completely changed. Today she held out her arms to Emerald and held her tightly, tears rolling down pale cheeks and sobs racking her body.

'I have been wanting to do this from the first second of meeting you again, my love,' she said when she had finally collected herself, her fingers entwined about Emerald's as they sat down.

'Again?' She had no memory of this woman in her life at all.

Blowing her nose soundly, Annabelle made an effort to continue. 'When you were five you came back to England and your mother and father brought you and your brother up to Knutsford to our house there.'

Emerald smiled. 'I remember my mother gave me

this locket. I remember a house high on a hill overlooking a river and a young boy…'

'Simon. My oldest child. He died of the ague in the Christmas of that same year. And then Evangeline was taken from us the following Easter.'

'She came home to England?'

'She was ill, Emerald. Ill with the depression of spirit, and drink was the only thing that made everything bearable.'

'Because she had killed my brother.'

Annabelle looked shocked. 'Beau told you that?'

'No. I remember it, though. James's broken body and my mother drunk against a wall with blood on her face.'

'He drowned, my dear. He wandered too near the sea and drowned. Evangeline jumped from the rocks into the water to try to save him and she never quite got over it when she could not. Your father sent her back to England to recover.'

'But she did not take me with her.'

'She could not take you. She hardly knew how to care for herself and Beau promised that he would bring you to England within the month. When the storms came early he had to wait and by then it was all too late. Your mother had gone back to her Maker and the first easy spoils of piracy had come Beau's way. There was no going back after that. I often wondered, if she had lived, would things have been different, though. I think her death took the heart from him.'

Emerald sat still and sifted the information through her mind, trying to make some sort of sense of all the recollections. Not a mad drunk woman after all, but a soul-saddened mother who had lost a child. For the first time ever she saw the faint ghost of Evangeline, smiling, beckoning, loving. Evangeline. A woman who had been transplanted into the tropics where the humidity had eaten at both her soul and her sanity. A fragile English rose blighted in the wilder soils of the Caribbean.

Now forgiveness crept in over anger, and an unfamiliar peace chased hard on the heels of a softer acceptance.

James. Beau. Evangeline. A family again in the hereafter. There was a rightness about it that made sense.

The relief was all encompassing.

When Annabelle handed her a small image of her parents, she saw exactly where it was that she had come from. Red-blonde curls and laughing turquoise eyes and dimples. Her mother. Her. Her fingers tightened on the likeness and she was pleased when Annabelle said that she might keep it.

'As family, you know that you would be most welcome to come to Longacres to live with me. With Miriam, of course and your little sister. Asher has told me she is a musical child?'

Emerald wanted to say yes, wanted to hold on to an offer that was both generous and unexpected. But she also knew that to be less than five miles from Falder would be a torture. To see Asher and not be with him, to watch from a distance the milestones in his life. A wife. Children. Grandchildren.

No, she knew absolutely and irrevocably that she could not do it.

'I thank you sincerely for your invitation, but at the moment…' She shook her head, finding it hard to convey in words the depth of her thanks.

'I understand things may be difficult, but, if you should change your mind for any reason, my offer would still stand. You will always be welcome at Longacres.'

When Annabelle had gone Emerald walked across the fields of Falder and towards the water, the breeze on her face cooling and the distant ocean beckoning from afar, a silver thread of ribbon. She mulled over Annabelle's offer and balanced it against the chancy hope of finding treasure. Perhaps she could take up the promise of a home for Miriam and Ruby…

She shook her head. Lord, to leave this place would be a wrench she could hardly bear the thinking of. Tucking her curls behind her ears, she pressed on towards the ocean. The tight squeeze of tears blurred her vision.

They met each other at the stream that bound the Wellingham land to the west before the road to Rochcliffe. Asher was on the same horse he always rode, a large black stallion with a streak of wildness in his blood. Like his owner, she thought, and waited as he dismounted. She knew he had returned to Falder very late in the night; she had heard the turn of wheels across the courtyard cobbles and heard the commotion the incoming vehicle had caused among the myriad servants.

This afternoon a quieter demeanour wreathed him as he said, 'Annabelle told me that she had talked to you. She said that she had asked you to stay at Long-acres with her, but that you had refused. She was at pains to understand why.'

'I need to go home to my sister.'

I need to get as far away from you as possible. From your eyes laced with gold, from the responsibility that sits so measured on your shoulders, from the promise of love that could only turn to hate, from the memory of your hands on my body in the night.

A quick glance at him made her blush.

'I want to show you something,' he said unexpectedly. 'It's this way.'

The thought flicked through Emerald's mind that perhaps he had followed her and had waited until she had come down into this valley. But why would he do that? He had made it plain that he did not want her company.

The thickness of trees evened out into farmland as they went, and ten minutes later a sharp outcrop of rock materialised above them.

'Here.' He beckoned and cut through a wedge of brambles. On the other side there was the mouth of a cave, hidden from view both by the hedges around it and by a large slice of rock that had sheared off from above.

She waited with him without talking for a moment by the entrance so that their eyes became accustomed to the dull light inside. And then she saw what it was that he wanted to show her. The walls on the far side were covered with figures, in red and ash and brown. Scenes of hunting and fighting and family, a thousand years of history hidden among the quiet hills of England.

'Taris and I discovered this place when we were boys. I've never told another person of its existence.'

'But you would tell me? Why?' Nothing made sense.

'When you were sick you told me your secrets. I felt it only fair to tell you some of mine.'

'Do you come here often?' She looked around, guessing the answer even before he gave it. A fur pelt lay on a raised platform constructed of wood in the middle of the room and a stool with a candle on top was beside it.

'After I came home and found Melanie had died, I made a bed down here. It was the only place I could gain a little sleep and at first—' he stopped '—at first it was the only place that I did not hear the voices.'

'Voices?'

'The voices in the compound at night when men were taken to…*hell.*' She could not imagine that she had heard him right until she saw the gleam of moisture in his eyes.

'Were you taken?'

'Yes.'

Anger winded her and then pain, for him, for them, for the truth and lies, and for lives changed by the curious whims of circumstance.

He held his right hand up to the light. The hand that was missing two fingers. 'It was a game to them, the mutilation of bodies, and some men lost a lot more than I did.'

'It is why you do not sleep?'

'Did not sleep. When you were in my bed I slept.'

The power of his words melted away restraint and she moved forward.

'Sleep with me, then. Here.' She did not waver, did not think, did not let the future take anything away from the sheer honesty of this moment, and when his thumb came up to trace the line of her jaw she closed her eyes and just felt.

Felt his hands on her bodice and her skirt. Felt the cold of air and then the warmth of fur. Felt the hard planes of his body and the hot thrust of his manhood. Close. Closer. Inside. Touching her heart. Taking her from the quiet dark confines of this place to heaven and back again and all under the watchful eyes of ancestors drawn in blood.

It was later, much later. Asher had lit a candle and pulled his jacket across them, the folds of wool warm in the chill of the early evening. Silence enveloped them, and timelessness, her cheek soft against the rise and fall of his chest.

'I think I know why you refused Annabelle's invitation when she offered you a home.'

She frowned and leaned back so that she could look at him.

'It's clairvoyancy you have the knack of, then?' She tried to sit up, but he would not let her.

'No, merely sense and reason. I think that you are afraid of staying here.'

His guess was so near the mark she was silent.

'And you are afraid of staying here because you are

so much more used to running, from your father, from the law, from your enemies. And the fact that in this little corner of England there could finally be a home for you is tempered with even more risk because you are Emerald Sandford, the pirate's daughter, and you are not prepared to chance it turning sour.'

Restraint broke as she wriggled out from the circle of his arms. 'That's right. I am afraid to stand by and let you see just how hated my family name is, to know just how many people Beau stole from or hurt or killed, because then, in place of what I see in your eyes now, would come something else and I don't want that something else. Not from you, Asher, not when I have had this.' The cold air in the cave against her nakedness made her shiver.

'Then fight them, damn it.'

'No. Don't you see? Don't you know? When life disappointed both my parents, they dissolved into pieces.' She was shouting so loud now that it hurt the soft tissue in the back of her throat. 'Pieces that tore apart reason and left only chaos. I feel that chaos inside me, sometimes, and wonder if I am just the same. What if I stay and ruin you and your family and Annabelle and Miriam…?'

In reply he stood and lifted her up against him, facing her towards a mirror she had not noticed before.

'What do you see?' he asked.

She did not understand.

'Small expressions, the line of your jaw, the colour of your eyes, the way your hair falls down just here, the mark of a knife on your brow.' His finger swept up and pushed back her heavy fringe. 'We are all the sum of what has come before us but we are also the beginning of what will come next. And in the middle stands choice, Emerald. The choice to be exactly who you want to become…here.' His hand fell to the place above her heart and she could feel the beat of her body echoed in his.

'You truly believe that?'

'I do.' The gold in his eyes was strong, intense. 'And it was you who taught me to do so with your courage and conviction. Together we could weather anything.'

'Together?'

'I will come with you to Jamaica to fetch your sister if you will give me a promise.'

She nodded and waited to see what he would say next.

'I want you to promise that you will return to Falder with me.'

'Return?'

'I won't let you go, Emerald. Ever. No matter what.'

The tears in the back of her eyes welled up when he drew her back into the bed beside him for in her acceptance of his lovemaking she knew that she would stay here in England as his mistress. And she had never quite imagined herself in such a role.

Chapter Seventeen

Emerald left England late on the evening tide and, as the land receded against the horizon, Asher's voice broke into her thoughts.

'We will be in Jamaica before next month's end.'

The gathering breeze whipped at his words and the sails above them caught and billowed.

Jamaica? As Asher's mistress? He had never mentioned marriage again, even in the aftermath of last night's lovemaking, and yet being at his side was enough. More than enough.

When he took her hand and led her down to the cabin they would share she followed him gladly, interested as they went in the layout of this ship. There was the galley and surgeon's cabin, to one corner of which was a bench well set out with medical supplies. The *Nautilus* would ride the oceans well, she thought, her lines both gracious and clean and her crew well looked after.

As they came to a heavy door, he stopped.

'Close your eyes.' His voice was husky and full of an anticipation she could not quite understand. When he led her inside she felt the warmth of the air and heard the quiet play of water around the hull. 'Now open them.'

A display of gowns hung in the wardrobe opposite her, shoes and shawls and undergarments in a variety of designs on the large table beside it. Crossing the room she ran a finger down the startling shot-red silk of a beautiful day dress.

'Madame Berenger was sure that they would fit you.'

'You bought these for me?'

He closed the door and came to stand beside her. Swallowing. Almost nervous?

'I thought that you needed them.'

'And she can make gowns without a fitting?'

'I described you. In detail.' His gaze ran across her, lazy, sensual, unhurried, and Emerald's heartbeat faltered. Was this the life of a kept woman, a constant flow of material goods in lieu of the payment for what she imagined would come next?

Suddenly she knew that she couldn't quite do it. Not without honesty anyway.

'I am not certain as to how long we will stay in the Caribbean, but there are some things about me that aren't… aren't…' Her mind scurried through an easier way to say what she needed to and she was glad for his continued silence.

'I am not accepted in any social circles there,' she blurted out, and when Asher stepped forward she stopped him.

'But you lived in the town?'

'We were outcasts.'

The anguish in the words was tangible, even to her. Lord, how she had wanted to be part of something, part of the village or the congregation in the church on the high hill overlooking the sea. Part of the picnics and gatherings at Easter and the joy of May Day celebrations. She had to explain it to him. Before they reached Kingston Town. Before he knew the exact extent of her damaged reputation.

'Even dressed in these, they would still know me.'

'Marry me then, Emerald.' His words were barely whispered, and she had to look up to see that he had indeed spoken.

'Marry you?'

'As the Duchess of Carisbrook, criticism would be far more muted and I have taken the liberty of bringing a parson aboard.' The pad of his thumb wiped the moisture from the soft skin on her cheek. 'I can protect you if you will let me.'

'Why?'

He turned and she saw the muscle in the side of his jaw ripple in tension.

'Because I love you.'

Had she heard him right? The warm strength of hope was like a drug, a heady elixir fed directly into the throbbing jugular at her neck. Could he possibly mean it?

'I've loved you ever since you bent over at the Bishop of Kingseat's party wearing nothing but skin underneath your gown.'

The gold in his eyes was brittle sharp. 'And I have thought about it many a night since.'

Unexpectedly she laughed, the sound fading away as he reached into his pocket to bring out a small box and flipped it open. An emerald ring sat in velvet, its true clear green catching the light from the lamp. Removing it, he caught at her left hand and placed the gold band on the third finger.

'Marry me, Emerald Sandford. Here on the ship. Before we reach Jamaica.'

And suddenly it was easy in the warmth of his embrace as his lips came down across hers to seal the bargain.

She would do it. She would marry him. Now. Today. His eyes were soft with passion and smouldering dark.

"I have something else for you too. Something that you lost in London.'

He leant across to the bureau beside him and brought out a box. Delight claimed her. Her pearls.

'How could you have known that they were mine?' she asked.

'I guessed. The initials. The place of purchase. The fact that Miriam's card was left as surety.'

'Evangeline chose them when I was a baby.'

'And now they are your wedding gift.'

Tears filled her eyes as she carefully laid the necklace in its box and stepped back to her satchel. Lifting out the map, she handed it across to Asher.

'As it is the time for new beginnings I would like to give you this.'

She saw surprise in the lines of his face and the tone in his voice was rough. 'I would waste neither time nor money chasing such a fickle promise.'

'I know.' Relief flooded her as he lifted the parchment and tore it into tiny fragments and when he was finished she let go of the breath she was unaware that she had taken.

It was over. Her old life. It was gone for ever and in the ashes of greed rose a phoenix of love, the bright possibility of a future with Asher replacing uncertainty with joy.

She touched the emerald. Not just any ring, after all, but hers.

'It's beautiful. Where did you get it?'

'I went to London when you began to recover. To a brothel in Curzon Street, a place designed to make men forget their…difficulties. I stayed less than the time it took to finish a brandy before going straight to my jeweller's.'

Emerald began to smile. And when she took his hands in her own she noticed that he was no longer wearing the sapphire on his little finger. She stroked the pale band of skin left beneath it and the ghosts of the past floated between them as he let out his breath.

'When Melanie died I knew, even in the darkest days of grief and guilt, that I would survive it. But if anything were to happen to you, Emerald, I know that I would not…'

She brought her finger across his lips to stop the words and he gathered her close and pulled her down into the softness of kapok, the ocean around them swelling soft and known.

Their world.

'I could stay here for ever,' she whispered.

One eyebrow cocked upward. Hopefully.

'Here in this bed?'

She began to laugh, but amusement faded as he undid the stays on her bodice and pushed the material back.

'You are so very beautiful. Your skin…the tattoo…' He traced around the edges of the mark, a frown across his forehead. 'A butterfly. *Mariposa* in Spanish. I should have guessed. All the time I should have known that it was you. My pirate wife.'

His arms took the weight as he rolled her beneath him, all humour long gone. 'I will never let you go, Emerald. This is for ever.'

'For ever,' she returned and welcomed the heat of his mouth as it slanted down hard across her own.

Epilogue

December 1823

The cold of winter was kept at bay by a roaring fire in the main hall of Falder.

Ruby sat to one side of Asher and in his lap their eight-month-old son slumbered, his soft breathing making Emerald smile.

'Play us another one, sweetheart,' Asher said as Emerald took the harmonica from her lips. 'It keeps Ashton quiet.'

Curling her fingers around the small instrument, she looked around. Lucinda and Rodney were ensconced in the corner and Miriam and Alice and Annabelle sat further over with tapestries on their knees, Azziz, Toro and Taris laughing behind them.

Her world.

Her world with Asher.

Full. Complete. Perfect.

She fingered the rich satin of her dress and her eyes caught the portrait above the fireplace. The portrait done last month by one of the painters now fashionable in society.

Emerald Wellingham, the Duchess of Carisbrook.

Asher had instructed the artist to draw the *Nautilus* dancing on the ocean, the rolling green hills of Falder behind and the peninsula of Return Home Bay.

And if she looked carefully she could see in the distance the outline of a ship that looked a lot like the *Mariposa,* a man and a woman and a young boy on the quarterdeck holding hands and smiling.

Tradition and the sweet fullness of family. The past bound finally into the present.

With love.

* * * * *

Enjoy a sneak preview of
MATCHMAKING WITH A MISSION
by B.J. Daniels,
part of the WHITEHORSE, MONTANA *miniseries.*
Available from Harlequin Intrigue
in April 2008.

Nate Dempsey has returned to Whitehorse to uncover the truth about his past...

Nate sensed someone watching the house and looked out in surprise to see a woman astride a paint horse just on the other side of the fence. He quickly stepped back from the filthy second-floor window, although he doubted she could have seen him. Only a little of the June sun pierced the dirty glass to glow on the dust-coated floor at his feet as he waited a few heartbeats before he looked out again.

The place was so isolated he hadn't expected to see another soul. Like the front yard, the dirt road was waist-high with weeds. When he'd broken the lock on the back door, he'd had to kick aside a pile of rotten leaves that had blown in from last fall.

As he sneaked a look, he saw that she was still there, staring at the house in a way that unnerved him. He shielded his eyes from the glare of the sun off the dirty window and studied her, taking in her head of long blond hair that feathered out in the breeze from under her Western straw hat.

She wore a tan canvas jacket, jeans and boots. But it was the way she sat astride the brown-and-white horse that nudged the memory.

He felt a chill as he realized he'd seen her before. In that very spot. She'd been just a kid then. A kid on a pretty paint horse. Not this one—the markings were different. Anyway, it couldn't have been the same horse, considering the last time he had seen her was more than twenty years ago. That horse would be dead by now.

His mind argued it probably wasn't even the same girl. But he knew better. It was the way she sat the horse, so at home in a saddle and secure in her world on the other side of that fence.

To the boy he'd been, she and her horse had represented freedom, a freedom he'd known he would never have—even after he escaped this house.

Nate saw her shift in the saddle, and for a moment he feared she planned to dismount and come toward the house. With Ellis Harper in his grave, there would be little to keep her away.

To his relief, she reined her horse around and rode back the way she'd come.

As he watched her ride away, he thought about the way she'd stared at the house—today and years ago. While the smartest thing she could do was to stay clear of this house, he had a feeling she'd be back.

Finding out her name should prove easy, since he figured she must live close by. As for her interest in Harper House... He would just have to make sure it didn't become a problem.

* * * * *

Be sure to look for
MATCHMAKING WITH A MISSION
and other suspenseful Harlequin Intrigue stories,
available in April
wherever books are sold.

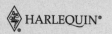

HARLEQUIN®

INTRIGUE®

❧ WHITEHORSE ❧
MONTANA

No matter how much Nate Dempsey's past haunted
him, McKenna Bailey couldn't keep him off her mind.
He'd returned to town to bury his troubled youth—
but she wouldn't stop pursuing him until he was
working on the ranch by her side.

Look for

MATCHMAKING
WITH A
MISSION

BY
B.J. DANIELS

*Available in April
wherever books are sold.*

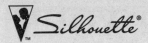

Romantic
SUSPENSE

**Sparked by Danger,
Fueled by Passion.**

The Taken

Tierney Doyle is used to being criticized for
her psychic abilities, yet the tough-as-nails—
and drop-dead-gorgeous—detective has no doubt
about what she has uncovered in the case of a
string of unsolved murders. And Tierney is slowly
discovering that working so close to her partner,
detective Wade Callahan, could be lethal.

Look for

Danger Signals
by Kathleen Creighton

Available in April wherever books are sold.

REQUEST YOUR FREE BOOKS!

Harlequin® Historical
Historical Romantic Adventure!

2 FREE NOVELS PLUS 2 FREE GIFTS!

YES! Please send me 2 FREE Harlequin® Historical novels and my 2 FREE gifts (gifts are worth about $10). After receiving them, if I don't wish to receive any more books, I can return the shipping statement marked "cancel". If I don't cancel, I will receive 6 brand-new novels every month and be billed just $4.94 per book in the U.S. or $5.49 per book in Canada, plus 25¢ shipping and handling per book and applicable taxes, if any*. That's a savings of 20% off the cover price! I understand that accepting the 2 free books and gifts places me under no obligation to buy anything. I can always return a shipment and cancel at any time. Even if I never buy another book, the two free books and gifts are mine to keep forever.

246 HDN ERUM   349 HDN ERUA

Name	(PLEASE PRINT)	
Address		Apt. #
City	State/Prov.	Zip/Postal Code

Signature (if under 18, a parent or guardian must sign)

Mail to the **Harlequin Reader Service:**
IN U.S.A.: P.O. Box 1867, Buffalo, NY 14240-1867
IN CANADA: P.O. Box 609, Fort Erie, Ontario L2A 5X3

Not valid to current subscribers of Harlequin Historical books.

Want to try two free books from another line?
Call 1-800-873-8635 or visit www.morefreebooks.com.

* Terms and prices subject to change without notice. N.Y. residents add applicable sales tax. Canadian residents will be charged applicable provincial taxes and GST. This offer is limited to one order per household. All orders subject to approval. Credit or debit balances in a customer's account(s) may be offset by any other outstanding balance owed by or to the customer. Please allow 4 to 6 weeks for delivery. Offer available while quantities last.

Your Privacy: Harlequin Books is committed to protecting your privacy. Our Privacy Policy is available online at www.eHarlequin.com or upon request from the Reader Service. From time to time we make our lists of customers available to reputable third parties who may have a product or service of interest to you. If you would prefer we not share your name and address, please check here. ☐

HH08

COMING NEXT MONTH FROM

HARLEQUIN®
HISTORICAL

- **KLONDIKE FEVER**
  by **Kate Bridges**
  (Western)
  Robbed at gunpoint, chained to a drifter, Lily thinks life can't get any
  worse—until she realizes that she's shackled to the one man she's never
  been able to forget!
  Don't miss the continuation of Kate Bridges's thrilling Klondike series!

- **NO PLACE FOR A LADY**
  by **Louise Allen**
  (Regency)
  Miss Bree Mallory has no time for the pampered aristocracy! She's
  too busy running the best coaching company on the roads. But an
  accidental meeting with an earl changes everything.
  Join Louise Allen's unconventional heroine as she shocks Society!

- **A SINFUL ALLIANCE**
  by **Amanda McCabe**
  (Tudor)
  Marguerite is exceptionally beautiful—and entirely deadly! Sent by a
  king to assassinate the gorgeous Nicolai, she finds herself torn between
  royal duty and ardent desire....
  *Award-winning Amanda McCabe brings us scandal and seduction at
  the Tudor court!*

- **THE WANTON BRIDE**
  by **Mary Brendan**
  (Regency)
  With disgrace just a breath away, Emily ached for Mark's strong arms
  to comfort her. Yet she held a secret—one that would surely prevent *any*
  gentleman from considering her as a suitable bride....
  *Can his passion overcome her fears? Find out in Mary Brendan's
  Regency tale.*